DEAD WICKED

A totally addictive crime thriller with a huge twist

HELEN H. DURRANT

DI Calladine & DS Bayliss Book 10

D0939900

JOFFE
BOOKS

First published 2020
Joffe Books, London
www.joffebooks.com

Please join our mailing list for free kindle crime thriller, detective, mystery, and romance books and new releases.

www.joffebooks.com/contact

ISBN 978-1-78931-454-0

For my favourite and only grandson – Jake (Jakey).

PROLOGUE

Closing time after a lock-in at the Pheasant. Kieron Ramsey staggered out of the pub into a pitch-black night and swore. The streetlights on the Hobfield Estate were a regular target for kids and the council had given up replacing them. He couldn't see a thing. His bleary eyes couldn't even make out the tower block he lived in. He stumbled along in the dark for a few yards, tripped and fell to his knees. He'd had a skinful, alright.

A pair of strong arms hauled Ramsey to his feet. "C'mon, mate, I'll give you a hand."

"County won at home, first time in ages," Ramsey slurred. "Don't drink as a rule, practically teetotal, but got carried away, didn't I? Not like me at all." He nodded in the direction of the towers. "I'm in Heron House. Just dump me at the entrance, thanks. I should have called it a day an hour ago, but that win needed celebrating. Christ, I feel bad." Ramsey bent double, hands on his knees. "Oh God, I'm going to throw up."

"Not 'ere." The man dragged him towards the waste ground where the tenants parked their vehicles.

Ramsey coughed, choking on the vomit rising in his throat. "Just get me home. I need my bed."

He was too drunk and out of it to realise that the man had led him to the far end of the waste ground well away from the towers, where a large dark-coloured van was parked up. When he finally saw where he was, he swung round protesting, his arms flailing as he tried to wrestle free. "Hey, mate, I need to go back that way."

The man held his arm in an iron grip and, drunk as he was, Ramsey couldn't loosen it. Instead, he poked the stranger in the chest. "Let me go home or you'll come off worst," he threatened. "I can make things difficult. You're forgetting, I know you and I know what you're up to. I've seen you in the—"

Cutting him off, the man launched a fist at him, hitting Ramsey hard on the mouth. "Shut it! You know nothing!" He opened the van doors, dragged him inside and threw him to the floor.

Ramsey lay coughing and spitting blood, struggling desperately to stand. When that failed, he reached into his pocket and pulled out his wallet. "You want money?"

The man kicked out, his foot thudding into Ramsey's belly. "No, mate. What I want is you silenced. I'm going to shut your mouth once and for all."

"You're mad, you. What am I s'posed to have said?"

"It's what you might say. I can't take the risk." He kicked Ramsey again, making him yelp. "I won't have you spoiling my plans by shouting your mouth off to that girl and anyone else who'll listen."

Kieron Ramsey wiped a grimy hand over his face. "Let me go. We can forget this. I won't say a word."

"Too right you won't."

Terrified, Ramsey tried to scramble away but was brought up short by a sharp kick to his shin. He didn't know what he'd done to deserve this. "Last chance. Release me and I'll go straight home. I won't tell a soul about tonight."

The man sneered. "Sorry, mate, no can do."

Ramsey saw the glint of a wicked-looking blade.

The man chuckled. "There'll be no more telling tales now, you little bastard. I'll stop that tongue of yours wagging, once and for all."

CHAPTER 1

Day 1

Tom Calladine straightened his tie, grimacing at the stranger that stared back at him from the mirror. He shook his head. "Look at me. I'm done up like a dog's dinner. God knows why I'm bothering. I just wish they'd leave me be. I liked my job as it was, I didn't ask to be made up to DCI."

Amy Dean appeared behind him. "You look good, the clothes go with the job. Give it time, you'll love it after a bit."

"I bloody won't," Calladine complained. "I can't sit in an office all day pushing paperwork around. I'll go off my head."

Calladine was a hands-on copper. He did investigations, solved crimes. The paperwork was someone else's job. This . . . *situation* he found himself in was a bloody nightmare.

Amy was chuntering at him from the kitchen. Calladine knew she had his best interests at heart, but she hadn't a clue. She'd no right interfering anyway. Amy was no longer his girlfriend, and she should keep her opinions about what was good for him to herself.

"It's a step up. You should be proud of yourself."

"There's nothing to be proud of, you know. I'm an *acting* DCI and I only got the job because Rhona Birch left in such a hurry." Birch had scuttled off like the very devil was after her, and Calladine still wasn't sure why. The problem was Chesworth's, not hers. Unless, of course, Birch had known all along that they had a bent chief super? She'd left a mere month ago but it seemed like an age. Since she'd gone, he'd been moved into her office. All very well, but it was down the corridor from the incident room, consequently he didn't feel part of the team any more. The others were still together — Ruth, Rocco and Alice — and he could hear them sharing jokes and gossip, discussing things he was no longer privy to. Calladine hated it.

"You can still get involved in the cases — the team needs you."

"That's tricky when you've got a mountain of paperwork covering your desk. Them upstairs never let up about the reports, the figures that need collating, not to mention the damn budgets. The work doesn't suit me, it's that simple."

"They want you to apply for the permanent position, Tom," she reminded him.

"Save them a lot of bother, that would, but they'll be disappointed. I want my old job back. I don't do change, not at my age."

Amy's face fell. She'd have been even more disappointed if she knew he'd already put in a request for exactly that.

"At least give it a bit longer," she suggested. "Then if you really can't hack it, have a word with that new chief super of yours."

"Quaid? I doubt he'll be much use. Oldston gets all his attention, Leesworth is a backwater for them. I bet it'll be weeks before he deigns to venture into our station."

Amy changed the subject. "I'm taking Zoe for her scan later. Do you want to meet us at the hospital?"

Calladine's daughter, Zoe, was pregnant. The biological father was Professor Julian Batho, the senior forensic scientist at the Duggan Centre. Zoe and her partner, Jo Brandon, had planned to go down the IVF route, but Julian had stepped in and offered to be the donor. He was Amy's nephew and her only close relative. Hence, Amy saw herself as a sort of "surrogate" granny. Zoe and Jo's plan had seemed a good idea at the time, but Calladine was fast coming to realise that it would have its drawbacks.

"I might, depends how the day goes," he replied.

"Your mobile's ringing," Amy said.

Calladine looked around and then saw it on the sideboard. The caller was DC Simon Rockliffe, nicknamed 'Rocco.'

"We've got a body, sir. I thought you'd want to know straight away. It was found on the waste ground at the back of the Hobfield." He paused. "Apart from what killed him, it looks bad — the poor bloke's been beaten and cut up about the face and chest."

"Have you rung Ruth?" Calladine asked.

"She's here already, talking to Natasha Barrington and her crew."

Okay, the paperwork could wait. This was far more important — and more suited to his talents. Decision made. "Give me ten minutes."

* * *

Calladine had no sooner parked up than Ruth Bayliss, his sergeant and friend, was at his side. "The poor sod isn't a pretty sight. I'd say we had a right nutter on our hands." She nudged him. "What you doing here anyway? Don't you have reports to write?"

"Probably." He chuckled. "Bet you're eaten up with jealousy, aren't you? I mean, my new role is such fun."

Calladine looked at the two tower blocks looming above them against a grey sky. Over the years this place had given him and the team a shedload of aggro. The tenants came and went, but nothing ever really changed. The Hobfield was a magnet for villains.

"Give over, Tom," Ruth said. "If you hate the job that much, do something about it. Tell the powers that be a few home truths. It's about time they realised that we need you on the shop floor."

"A letter has been sent." He winked. "And you're right, the shop floor suits me just fine. Do we know how he died?"

"He was covered in mud and blood, so Natasha says it's difficult to tell. But among other things, they cut his tongue out." She shuddered. "Thing is, Natasha reckons he wasn't dead when it was done. She can't be sure until the PM, but given he was found on his back in that ditch, she thinks he might have choked to death on the blood."

Calladine grimaced. "Do we know who he is?"

"There's not much on him, no wallet or mobile, but he is local. We found a key in his pocket. I recognise it — it's from the tower block flats. They all have the same logo on them."

"Get uniform to knock on a few doors, find out who's missing." He turned and glanced back at the Pheasant. "Get them to ask in there too."

Calladine donned a pair of plastic overshoes and gloves and made his way to the tent that had been erected over the body.

Dr Natasha Barrington, the Home Office pathologist, met him at the entrance. "Whoever did this really went to town. Besides the other damage, the killer finished the job by cutting out the victim's tongue. The blood loss from that will have been great, but he still had the strength to attempt to escape. Forensics will check, but I think he staggered that way, and fell into the ditch that runs around the perimeter over there. We've had a lot of rain recently so it's full of water. That's where he was found. God knows how he managed to move at all, Tom. He'd been badly beaten, was bleeding heavily and unable to call for help. He'd be within seconds of dying. It must have been his final stab at making a run for it. At that point he was surviving on pure adrenalin."

"Desperate measures."

"There are also lots of deep cuts on his upper body made with a sharp blade. I suspect the same one was used to cut off his tongue."

"Have you found the tongue?" Calladine asked.

"No, perhaps the killer took it as a trophy. There's no sign of the weapon either."

Calladine peered into the tent at the remains. "Nasty. I wonder who he upset." The detective didn't recognise the victim, but then he wouldn't. His face was covered in mud from the ditch, and blood. This was way over the top. Calladine wasn't aware of any feuds going on around the estate at the moment. But if the victim was local, that meant the killer probably was too.

"Where was he attacked? Out here in the open?"

"Julian's team are doing a search. We can't find any blood on the ground, so not here. All we have to go on is the body in the ditch."

"Tortured and tongue cut out elsewhere, then," Calladine said.

"I would say so. Can we take him to the Duggan now?" Natasha asked.

Calladine nodded. "PM?"

"I'll do a preliminary examination once we get back. You're welcome to attend."

"Thanks, Natasha."

CHAPTER 2

Gina Haigh worked in Leesdon's one and only supermarket. Despite having to do just a few hours Saturday mornings and alternate days after college, she hated it. The work was boring, and the manageress, Joan Radcliffe, picked on her. The criticism was continual and usually concerned her hair, which was short, spiky, and currently coloured black and vivid green. But what made matters worse was that the jibes were not restricted to work. At home, Gina's aunt wasn't shy about sharing her views on the girl's appearance either. Between the two of them they made her life a misery.

Gina stood outside the supermarket rear entrance smoking a crafty fag with her workmate, Kelly. "Radcliffe's doing my frigging head in," she said. "You heard her, Kel, she never lets up."

"You could tone it down, G, just for work. That hair colour is a bit full-on, and this week you've done your nails to match."

Gina glanced down at them. To her eyes they looked great, alternating between green and black. She took a long pull on her fag, threw it to the ground and stamped on it. "Why should I? Madam in there needs to get a life, stupid witch. I'll paint myself up any way I want."

"Only saying, G. But carry on and she'll find an excuse to sack you."

"I do my job — she's got no beef there."

"There've been complaints. I heard her gossiping to that busybody from the flats. She said you look scary, like something done up for Halloween."

Gina folded her arms and leaned against the wall, her young face pulled into a frown. It was always this way. She was a flaw in the system, an anomaly, clever but difficult. Gina didn't like authority, and when you were in care there was plenty of that. Up until six months ago when her aunt took her on, she'd had half a dozen sets of foster parents, all of them unable to cope with her. She *was* different — her hair, her clothes and her attitude made her stand out, and people didn't like it. "I'm thinking of leaving anyway. This place is for losers."

Kelly put her nose in the air. "Thanks for that, G. I'm stuck here permanently. It's alright for you — you only do a few shifts. We don't all have someone who'll fund us through college, you know."

"I practically fund myself, and that bitch I live with isn't a parent, she's my mum's sister, stuck-up cow that she is. She's a do-gooder, wants those tossers in her church to see her in a good light. Well, another year and I'll be eighteen, then I'm out of there anyway."

"I still say you're lucky. You earn and you keep the lot. I work here all week and my mum demands half my wages. You don't live in the real world, G. You really are one spoilt bitch at times."

Gina was sick and tired of all the jibes. "Stuff it, I'm off. Tell Radcliffe what you like."

"Your bag's in the locker," Kelly said.

Gina followed Kelly inside, intending to collect her belongings and leave quietly, but all hell had broken loose in the supermarket. A crowd had gathered round a little lad in his buggy. He was clutching a carton of juice, throwing up and crying his eyes out. The woman with him was screaming, "My son's been poisoned!"

Gina didn't doubt that this was the truth. This was bad. "I'm not hanging around. Next thing, the place will be full of coppers. I'm out of here right now."

Joan Radcliffe approached the two friends. "There's an ambulance on its way. The mother bought that drink in here a few minutes ago. Get the rest of those cartons off the shelves, now!" She turned away, back to the woman.

"Sorry, Kel, I'm off. This will get nasty."

"You look scared, G. What's going on? Is this your doing?"

Gina saw the look of suspicion. "What d'you take me for? Course it's not."

"But you know something. It's written all over your face."

"Drop it, will you? Radcliffe asks, I've left 'cos I'm not well."

* * *

"The Duggan Centre?" Ruth Bayliss was driving Calladine away from the scene.

Calladine nodded. "This one will be grim. The poor bugger must have suffered. We've had nothing like this in a while. I must be getting old, I'm not sure if I can stomach this little lot for much longer."

"You can sit on the fence if you'd rather. The DCI job's waiting."

"Stuff that, I'd rather just grit my teeth."

Ruth changed the subject. "How's Zoe?"

"Pregnant, as you know, and fed up of all the attention she's getting from Amy and Julian."

"I thought she and Jo wanted Julian to be a part of the child's life? Amy will be going home soon, back to Cornwall."

"I'm not so sure. She's talking about staying until after the birth. She reckons that Julian will need help."

"That's not her call to make. Zoe and Jo are the parents, it'll be them raising the child."

Calladine huffed. "Try telling Amy that."

"Oh dear. I see problems on the horizon, and you'll be piggy in the middle," Ruth teased. "How are you and Amy getting on anyway?"

Calladine turned and stared out of the window. How to answer that one? His history with women wasn't good, his past was littered with broken relationships, mostly down to his inability to commit. Amy was a past dalliance that had ended when she'd chosen to leave him and move to Cornwall. He liked her, enjoyed her company, but that was as far as it went. Currently she was staying with him, a situation he was growing tired of, particularly as she wasn't shy of voicing her opinions on his career.

"Amy is okay in small doses, but she does try to take over. She forgets that we're not a couple any more."

Ruth grinned. "End of that particular road then?"

"Too true it is. I'm tired of trying to keep the peace. She's bought stuff for the baby and not even consulted Zoe and Jo. Zoe's got a scan today and Amy reckons she's going too. That won't go down well."

"Is Julian likely to turn up?"

"Who knows?" Calladine said. "But Zoe will not want a crowd, that much I'm sure of. Things change from week to week. Perhaps it's hormones but Zoe's not happy, I can see it in her face. Whether it's Julian, Amy or something else, she's not saying. I was round there at the weekend and Jo told me that all Zoe wants is to be left alone, she says she feels like an exhibit in a zoo."

CHAPTER 3

Leesworth police used the Duggan Centre to carry out post-mortems and for all the rest of their forensic needs. Dr Natasha Barrington, the pathologist, was brilliant at her job and the team trusted her judgement. The senior forensic scientist and investigator was Professor Julian Batho. He and Natasha worked together well, and between them had been responsible for finding the evidence that had allowed Calladine to solve many cases.

Calladine had known Julian for years. At one time Julian had been engaged to a member of Calladine's own team, Imogen Goode. When Imogen had met an untimely death in the course of her job, it had hit Julian hard. Offering to donate his sperm so Zoe and Jo could have a child was some compensation for him. Calladine knew that the serious-minded young man would invest both time and emotion in the child, if its parents would only let him. If she really wanted Julian to be a part of her child's life, Zoe would have to come to terms with that.

The detectives were ushered into the room where a technician was busy preparing the body. Julian was sifting through the victim's clothing. He had a man with him that Calladine hadn't seen before.

"This is Dr Rob Harris, our latest recruit," Julian said.

Harris nodded a greeting. He was blond, well built and tall. Calladine put him at around his late thirties.

"Are you from round here?" Ruth asked.

"Halifax, over the tops," he said. "I've been working at Leeds University but when this post came up, it was too good an opportunity to pass up. I was incredibly lucky to get it." He smiled.

"Rob's being too modest," Julian said. "His credentials are excellent, it's us that are the lucky ones."

Julian didn't often dole out praise like that. He'd obviously taken to Rob.

"Leesworth isn't that different from the area around Halifax — lots of hills and dodgy weather." Ruth smiled.

"I'm sure I'll settle in. I've got myself a little flat by the canal. Once I get things straight, you must all come round for a drink."

Evidently anxious to get back to business, Julian cleared his throat. "We'll look closely at the clothes. With luck they might give us something. The jacket he was wearing has what looks like paint flecks on the back of it. Also, I've had a look at the piece of wasteland near the ditch he was found in. I don't think that's where he was killed, there's no blood on the ground." He pushed his heavy-rimmed glasses up his nose and checked his watch. "I have to leave soon," he said. "If you have any questions after the PM, ask Rob. He will be working closely with me on this one."

"The scan?" asked Calladine. "Only, er, it might be wise to leave the girls to it this time. Zoe appreciates your—"

"She's asked me to be there," Julian said. "She's just sent me a message to remind me of it. You forget, Zoe, Jo and I had an agreement. Back at the beginning we decided to do this together. I know I can be a bit full-on, but I worry, that's all."

Calladine knew from experience that it was no use arguing with Julian. This child meant a lot to him, it gave him someone to focus on besides Imogen. Best leave him to it. "Ring Rocco, see if we have an ID yet," he said to Ruth.

Natasha joined them, gowned up and ready. "I can save you a job there," she said. "When he arrived, there was a lot of dried blood on his face, neck and chest from the wound to his tongue. Once we'd cleaned him up, one of the technicians here recognised him. Our technician used to work at the hospital with a Dr Bridge. Our victim was on the doctor's asthma trial. I know Howard Bridge and I've rung him and he's given me the victim's details." She nodded at the corpse. "His name is Kieron Ramsey."

Calladine nodded. "Thanks."

"Now, let's see what we've got."

The white sheet was removed to reveal a tall, thin young man whose upper body was covered in cuts and bruises, evidence of the beating and torture he'd suffered.

"The killer didn't hold back," Ruth observed.

"Given his injuries, I'm surprised he had the strength to attempt to escape," Natasha said.

"He'd be in a hell of a state," Ruth added. "The poor bugger must have been in agony."

"I want to check what is going on in his throat. If there are blood clots, it will reinforce the theory that he choked to death. Mind you, he does have a sizeable bump on the back of his head," Natasha said.

"Could that have been fatal?" Calladine asked.

"Incapacitating and serious, but I doubt it killed him." Natasha made some incisions to allow her to look at the back of his mouth and the oesophagus. Taking a large pair of tweezers, she went in. "Not quite what I thought," she said, and lifted something out. "The killer cut out the tongue and then pushed it back down his throat." She plopped the discoloured piece of flesh into a bowl. "The bang on the head was possibly the killer's way of rendering the poor man incapable of fighting back."

Ruth turned away, horrified by what had been done to the young man.

"Was he alive when he lost his tongue?" asked Calladine.

"Yes, hence all the blood. And he ran, don't forget. No doubt he was desperately trying to breathe through the blood flowing into his airway."

"Cause of death choking, then?" asked Calladine.

"Asphyxiation, and blood loss," Natasha said.

"What about the other wounds?"

"The bruising and cuts to his face and torso are ante-mortem. His body looks as if the murderer lost it and hacked at him wildly with a sharp blade."

Calladine had witnessed countless post-mortems over the years, but this was one of the worst. Seeing what had been done to the man, imagining how it must have been at the end, he decided Ruth was right — they had a nutter on their hands.

Once the PM was complete, Natasha cleaned up and sat at her laptop. "I have Ramsey's address for you." She handed Calladine a sheet of paper.

"Thanks. We'll need to tell his family, if he has any. We also need Ramsey's place going over with a fine-tooth comb."

"I'll get the team on it right away," Rob said.

Calladine knew nothing about this young man's work. He could only hope that he was as good as Julian thought. This was no time for Julian to do his prima donna act. They had a vicious killer to catch.

* * *

"Want to go to the station, fill the others in, perhaps get some coffee?" Ruth asked. "That was harrowing. A short break will do no harm."

"No, we should crack on while the trail is hot. I want this psycho catching quickly."

"Okay, Ramsey's flat it is then. I'll drive," Ruth said.

They headed for Heron House on the Hobfield, Calladine quiet and thoughtful in the passenger seat. Finally, he said, "Julian should oversee this, but he's too wrapped up with the baby. He's got it into his head that things aren't right, so he's going to the scan. It'll be nonsense put there by Amy. I wish she'd cut the psychic crap — it isn't doing him any good at all."

When Calladine had first met Amy Dean, she'd owned a 'new age' shop in Leesdon. She went by the name 'Amaris' and purported to be a fortune-teller. She'd helped the team on a case and in the course of it, she and Calladine had become involved. Amy was unconventional, both in her dress and her beliefs. Calladine couldn't get his head round half the things she told him, nor did he believe them. She might be Julian's aunt, but the two of them were poles apart. Julian was a scientist, with a scientist's worldview, but a little time spent with Amy and that world was falling apart.

"Julian speaks well of Rob. He's picky, don't forget, so I'd say he has to be one of the best. I think we can trust him," Ruth said.

Calladine smiled. "Dr Harris has won you over, then."

"What's not to like? He's well qualified, comes with Julian's recommendation and, well, he is rather dishy."

"Now we're getting to it. You're forgetting you're spoken for, Ruth Bayliss. What would Jake say? Dishy, indeed. I didn't expect that from you."

"Get over yourself, Calladine. He is dishy. Jake's okay, we muddle through, but Jake can be a bore at times. You know we've had our ups and downs. You've heard me complain often enough. I am still young, you know. Sometimes I quite fancy a bit of excitement. I think our relationship is getting stale. We've had our problems and we've tried to sort them, but things aren't getting any better."

"Well, liven the relationship up then — do something, organise a holiday, whatever!"

She snorted. "Says the expert on relationships!"

"Okay, let's drop it. The bottom line is, I don't want you getting hurt. Split with Jake and that's exactly what will happen. I'm looking out for you, that's all."

Ruth patted his arm. She knew he had her best interests at heart, but he could be wrong this time. "Okay, appreciated, but don't stick your nose in my private life, Calladine. I try to keep well out of yours."

"Don't be swayed, that's all. He's just a pretty face," he said. "You've too much to lose."

Ruth changed the subject. "I don't recognise Ramsey's name, and we know most of the troublemakers on the Hobfield."

"Because his name hasn't come up means nothing. He could be one of the rare ones, you never know, but he certainly upset someone. Perhaps Kieron owed money for drugs, or to a loan shark." Calladine shrugged. "But whatever the reason, the killer is one dangerous bastard."

Ruth's mobile rang. The caller was DC Alice Bolshaw, another member of the team.

"There's been an incident, ma'am," she said. "At the supermarket on the High Street. A child has been poisoned. Whatever he ingested was in a drink bought from the shop. A uniformed PC attended, and he reported that the carton had been tampered with, plus about a dozen more."

"How's the child?" Ruth asked at once. She had a small son of her own and could understand how worried the parents must be.

"He's in the hospital. We haven't had an update yet."

"Have you spoken to the manager? Have there been any threats made?" Ruth said.

"The manager is called Joan Radcliffe, and she has no idea why this has happened."

"One of you go and speak to the staff, they may be able to tell you something useful. We also need all the information you can find on one Kieron Ramsey. Thanks, Alice, keep me updated."

"Trouble?" Calladine asked.

"As if we didn't have enough! A case of poisoning at the supermarket. A child is in hospital and there could be more. I know we're busy, but we'll have to investigate, Tom. We'll start by speaking to the staff. With luck the culprit will turn out to be one of them. Otherwise, we could be looking at something big."

"What d'you mean?" he asked.

"Blackmail, disgruntled customer on a mission, who knows? But it needs sorting out quickly — the whole town shops there."

CHAPTER 4

Gina Haigh had to get away. The poisoning incident in the supermarket was the final straw. The people there didn't trust her, and she got the blame for most things that went wrong. If she wasn't around, there'd be no more trouble, hence no more earache. It was that simple.

She'd lied to her aunt, said she was off to stay with a friend for a few days, but her aunt wouldn't care anyway, Moira Haigh was too wrapped up in that business of hers. Besides, her aunt thought Gina was difficult to control, volatile and the cause of most arguments in the household. Well, not any more. Gina was done with all that. From now on, she'd please herself. Her boyfriend Arron Cookson, or 'Cooksie,' had offered her a way out. He knew someone with a caravan on the east coast. He said they could go there, chill, work things out and be free of the verbal flak for a while.

Gina checked the time on her mobile. The train was late. Gina was heading for Leeds and then on to Bridlington. She was about to put her phone back in her pocket when a message flashed on the screen. Her heart sank. Cooksie couldn't make it. He had a job to do for Noah. Great!

Gina texted back, *What job?*

Best you don't know, but I have no choice, you know Noah. The man's an animal and he's threatened to make serious trouble for us both. Anyway, this is a chance to make the money we need to be free of this lot at last.

She knew what that meant, more robbing and dealing around the estate, and now Cooksie would be in it up to his neck. That's what the supermarket incident would have been about — Noah letting them know that he held all the cards.

Noah Ash was a villain. He didn't live on the Hobfield but he still ran the estate, and was a law unto himself. He was backed up by a gang of hard nuts, not the sort you crossed. Cooksie had obviously attracted his attention, and now he was getting to him through her. Why not? It was a clever plan and it had worked.

Cooksie texted that she could get the key to the caravan they were staying in from the park reception, and he'd join her in a couple of days. Gina hated the idea of Cooksie being forced to do Noah's dirty work and was tempted to stand her ground, give him an earful, ditch the whole idea and stay in Leesdon, but what then? Noah was a vicious bastard and Gina didn't want another incident like the one at the supermarket. Also, her auntie would have heard about it by now and be on her case too. She rang her friend Kelly. She got straight to the point. "Make sure all the stock is checked, Kel, it's important."

"What's this about, G? What have you done?"

Gina didn't reply. She didn't know what to tell her. But Kelly wasn't stupid, she had to give her something and didn't want to involve Cooksie. "I've upset someone, a dealer," she lied. "I owe him money and I can't pay. The thing at work was him flexing muscle, letting me know he's got the upper hand. That's why I've got to leave. If I stay, he won't let up."

"Do you mean Noah Ash? You do, don't you? That monster's got something on you. You must go to the police, G," Kelly said. "Let them deal with him."

"Then what? You know Noah, he won't let things lie. His parents have money, they'll get him the best lawyers and he'll walk. No, Kel, it's better if I just do one for a while.

Do what I say, check everything and don't say a word to Radcliffe. I'll text her tomoz, say I'm ill or something."

The train pulled into the platform. Gina picked up her rucksack and stepped on. She sat at a window seat, mobile in hand, carefully deleting all messages and contacts that had anything to do with Leesdon, including those of her aunt and Kelly. She took a brand-new pay-as-you-go mobile from her pocket, transferred Cooksie's number onto it, and threw the old one in her rucksack. She'd dump it somewhere later. This was it. She'd done it now. There was no going back.

* * *

As Calladine and Ruth arrived at Heron House, the forensics team pulled up behind them. "Keen, isn't he, that Rob? Julian will have to watch his back. I smell ambition." Calladine smiled.

"Nothing wrong with that. He's probably got a plan, and I don't expect it involves hanging around Leesworth for too long either," Ruth said.

"Don't be so sure. Getting to work with Julian is a definite plus. Our Julian might seem like an oddball to us, but he's well known and admired in forensics circles. I bet there are plenty of hopefuls who'd love the chance to work with him."

Ruth laughed. "Don't tell Julian, whatever you do. He's opinionated enough as it is!"

Kieron Ramsey had lived alone in a flat on the tenth floor of Heron House. Peering amid the crowd of forensic investigators, Ruth could see that the place was spick and span. Kieron Ramsey seemed to have been unnaturally tidy for a young single man.

"Searching this little lot should be a breeze," she noted, opening a drawer. "Everything is stacked in neat little piles. Look at the kitchen, nothing out of place."

"Perhaps he had a touch of OCD. It'll make forensics' job easier." Calladine nodded at the coffee table. "His mobile. We'll take that."

Rob Harris approached them. "We've started the search but so far found nothing of interest — no drugs, no suspicious mail. There was no mobile on the body, so I presume it's the one on the table. He must have left it behind when he went out."

"We'll check the providers, see what calls he made and received. Might give us something," Ruth said.

Calladine put on a pair of gloves and tried to switch the mobile on. "It's password protected," he said with irritation.

"Do you want us to check it for prints?" Rob Harris asked. "We can pass it onto IT forensics after that," he added. "They'll check his browser history and that."

"No need," Calladine said. "Ramsey didn't have it on him when he was killed, so we'll deal with it."

Ruth was upstairs, checking on the bedrooms.

"Anything up there?" Calladine shouted up to her.

"Not that I can see," Ruth said. "A few clothes in the wardrobe, everything is neat and tidy in the drawers and the bathroom cabinet contains nothing but soap and shampoo. I can't find anything that would make him a target for a killer." She moved around, looking at every surface. "There's not even a photo, or a magazine. It's weird, as if he didn't really live here at all."

"He was tidy — there are worse things to be," Calladine said, as she re-joined them downstairs.

"I'm sure forensics will bottom the place." She smiled at Rob. "There could be drugs hidden somewhere, for example. That's a good way to get killed around here. And there has been dealing on the estate recently."

"I've seen no sign of drugs or anything else incriminating," Rob said, returning her smile. "But it is my intention to let the dogs have a sniff around once we've finished."

"There has to be something, the poor bloke wasn't just killed for no reason. Whoever did that to him had a point to make. That attack was way over the top." Calladine checked his mobile and found a message from Zoe. She'd attached an

22

image of the scan. Beaming proudly, he passed it to Ruth. "My first grandchild."

Ruth grinned. "Cute little blob."

He gave her a look of mock outrage. "How dare you, Sergeant Bayliss. That's no blob, it's a little Calladine."

The pair almost missed the knock on the door they were laughing so much. A woman was calling from the doorway. "Is Kieron here?"

Both detectives spun round to look at her. She was tall, with blonde hair tucked into a neat plait at the back of her head, tendrils framing her face and highlighting her delicate features. She was wearing a straight skirt and jacket in dark colours.

Calladine was temporarily stunned. For one moment he thought he was looking at a ghost. The woman was a dead ringer for Lydia Holden. He couldn't speak, but simply stood and stared. How was this possible? Lydia had been the love of his life at one time, but she was *dead*.

"Who are you?" Calladine asked finally, flashing his warrant card.

She took an identity card from her bag and showed it to them, smiling. "Emma Holden. I'm a social worker, focusing on looked-after children, and Kieron used to be one of my cases before I moved away. Kieron's not like most young men of his age. He doesn't make friends easily, doesn't fit in. He trusts me, and over time we've built a bond, so whenever I'm in the area I visit, just to make sure he's okay."

"Why was he in care?" Ruth asked.

Ignoring Ruth's question, Calladine asked, "Holden? Are you related to Lydia?"

She looked at him, puzzled. "Lydia was my sister. Did you know her?"

He smiled. "Yes. It's possible she mentioned me. I'm Tom."

The puzzlement gave way to a look of recognition. "Tom Calladine? Yes, she did speak about you. You were close."

Ruth nudged him. This wasn't what they were here for. "Tell us about Kieron," she said.

"I keep an eye, ensure he's settled and working. During the time I've known him, Kieron hasn't been easy to deal with, but of late, he seems to have got himself sorted."

"I'm afraid he's been murdered," Calladine said gently. "He was found on that patch of waste ground out there."

The woman turned pale. "I don't understand. He was a quiet, inoffensive young man — mind you, get a drink inside him and sparks flew. He couldn't handle it, you see. Had he been fighting? I only saw him last weekend and he told me everything was fine."

"Does he have relatives in the area?" Ruth asked. "We need to find out as much as we can about his friends and any family, where he went and if he'd upset anyone."

"There's no family left," the woman said. "Kieron was in care from the age of five. His parents were killed when he was a small child. The only family he had then was an ageing aunt, so there was no one to take him on. She used to visit him and kept in touch until she died about eight years ago."

"Would you be prepared to formally identify the body?" Ruth asked. "We found nothing on him. When he arrived at the Duggan Centre one of the pathologist's assistants recognised him. They'd been on some medical trials together some months ago."

"The asthma trial." She sighed. "Okay, I suppose I'll have to." Emma Holden gave Calladine a long hard look. "Lydia couldn't make you out. She left Leesdon because she didn't know if you loved her or not. If she'd stayed, perhaps she'd still be alive."

The words stung. Calladine had thought about Lydia a lot since her death, and her sister was right. If she'd stayed, she might still be alive. "That's not how it was," he insisted. "What we had simply came to an end."

"Whatever, but she isn't here to tell her side, is she?"

CHAPTER 5

Rocco spent the afternoon gathering all the information he could find on Kieron Ramsey. Their victim was twenty-three years old and had lived in Leesdon since leaving Maple House children's home in Oldston at age eighteen. He was local, however — his parents and grandparents had lived in Leesdon before him. He wasn't workshy. Since leaving school he'd worked at the local supermarket, and at the time of his murder was on their management training programme. It wasn't lost on Rocco that this was the supermarket where the little lad had been poisoned earlier. Were the two incidents connected?

"Our victim from this morning worked in Leesdon supermarket," he told Alice. "How's that for a coincidence?"

"Calladine doesn't believe in coincidence and neither do I," she said.

"I'm off there now. D'you know it at all? Friendly, are they?"

"I shop there. The manageress is a bit grim, stern-faced and barking orders all the time. The staff always look scared stiff when she's around."

"What d'you reckon this morning was about?"

Alice looked up from the report she was working on. "I'm not sure. Samples and several other cartons have gone off to the lab. We'll have to see what comes back. It could be down to a customer with a grudge perhaps? Or something more personal against Ramsey in particular, someone certainly didn't like him. None of this will do the supermarket's reputation any favours. I, for one, will think twice before shopping there again."

Rocco nodded. "You don't think the kid simply threw up his breakfast then?"

"His mother was certain he'd drunk something poisonous, and she said it was in the carton of juice she'd just bought."

"Weird, though, both incidents — the murder and the poisonings — connected to the same place."

"Given Ramsey's murder, it does smack of someone with a score to settle," Alice said. "While you're gone, I could take a look at the manageress's background, see what comes up?"

"Thanks, Alice, that would be useful." He grabbed his stuff and sent a quick text to Ruth, telling her where he'd gone.

Leesdon supermarket was at the end of the High Street, set a little way back with a large parking area. Rocco passed it on his way home most days, but he'd never shopped there.

Joan Radcliffe was in her office at the back of the store. An assistant showed Rocco in and he introduced himself.

"The child is fine," she said at once. "Whatever he swallowed hasn't done him any lasting harm."

That was good news, at least. "I'm actually here about another matter," he began.

"Not the poisoning?"

"There has been another incident, more serious. A member of your staff, Kieron Ramsey, has been murdered. His body was found this morning."

Joan Radcliffe turned pale. "Murdered?" she said in a shocked whisper. "Are you sure? I can't imagine who would do such a thing! Kieron wasn't the type who upset people. He was a kind, hardworking young man. He was always smart and on time, everyone liked him. He had a promising career with this company. I didn't know much about his personal life, but I wasn't aware of any problems."

"We do need to find out more about him. We've been told there's no family. Was he friendly with anyone here in particular?"

"Gina." She frowned. "I did warn him that she was trouble. That could be your answer. She has a boyfriend with a dubious background." She shook her head. "Gina has trouble written all over her. The way she dresses, the make-up she plasters on her face, not to mention the hair! And she mixes with a right rough bunch. Kieron liked her, but she just wasn't his type. I'm not aware of there being any trouble between them though."

"Can I speak to her?" Rocco asked.

Joan Radcliffe lowered her gaze. "Gina hasn't turned up for work this afternoon. In fact, she left in a hurry while we were dealing with that child earlier, and she hasn't been back since. Another member of staff said she was ill, but I have my doubts."

"Can I have Gina's details, please?"

"Yes, of course, but be warned, her Aunt Moira won't be happy. Gina has no parents and now lives with her. The two are constantly at odds. Mind you, that's not difficult with Gina. She is something of an acquired taste. I only took her on because Moira Haigh is a friend of mine."

"Do you have CCTV inside the shop?" Rocco asked.

"Yes, but it's pointed towards the tills."

"If you sort out the footage for the day before the incident and that morning, we'll take a look anyway."

"I'll make sure you have it before you leave," she said.

"The other staff, could I speak to them?"

"Yes, of course. You can use this office," Radcliffe said. "I'll leave you to it and I'll send them in one at a time. Gina was friendly with Kelly Munroe, so I'll send her in first."

Kelly Munroe turned out to be a pretty nineteen-year-old. She was obviously very nervous and kept casting furtive looks behind her as Rocco asked her to sit down.

"You look frightened, Kelly. Are you okay?" he began.

"I've never been interviewed by the police before," she said. "Is this about Gina?"

"Partly, but mostly it's about Kieron Ramsey. He's been murdered."

The girl looked at him, open-mouthed.

"After the incident with the child," Rocco went on, "Gina left in a hurry. She didn't wait around to answer any questions. Do you have any idea why that might be?"

Kelly shrugged. "She won't have harmed Kieron if that's what you're getting at. She couldn't. They were friends, and I doubt if G would harm anyone. She talks the talk, but that's all it is."

"What about the poisoning? Do you think she had anything to do with that?" he asked.

Kelly averted her eyes. "I don't know, but it frightened her, I do know that."

"Is that why she went missing?"

"It could be. She's had a lot of warnings from her auntie about her behaviour. Gina gets the blame for most things that go wrong at home and here. It's not fair. She speaks her mind and people don't like it. Perhaps she thought if the police went round to the house again, her auntie would freak."

"Were Kieron and Gina close?"

"Not really. He was soft on her and I know he'd asked her out, but G wasn't having any of it. He just wasn't her type. But she let him down gently, they got on, looked out for each other. Besides, Gina has a boyfriend."

"Can I have his name?"

"Cooksie — Arron Cookson. He lives on the Hobfield, but I don't know where exactly."

"Is Cookson the jealous type?" Rocco asked.

"I hardly know him, but he is into Gina, I know that."

"Thanks, Kelly."

Rocco spent the next hour speaking to the other supermarket staff but learned very little, except that Gina wasn't liked. Both her colleagues and the customers were wary of her and tended to give her a wide berth. As he was about to leave, Joan Radcliffe handed him Gina's address and a memory stick. "The footage is on there."

"Do you know if Gina knew the little boy who was ill, or his mother?" Rocco asked.

"I don't know. The woman never said anything. She was very upset. If she thought it was deliberate, I'm sure she would have said so."

Rocco decided he'd speak to her anyway. He'd get her details from the station.

CHAPTER 6

You are trying my patience. Moira Haigh read the text and a shiver of fear went through her. She was running out of options.

I suggest you pay up, make things easy on yourself. That way you get your system back and your business can continue as before.

Moira had been duped. The email had looked innocent enough, exactly like so many others that dropped into her inbox during the working day. Her days were busy enough as it was, without having to weed through potential scam communications.

You want your system back, have access to your accounts and everything else you need to run your business, pay up and I'll make this nonsense go away.

But it wasn't nonsense, it was very real. Moira's entire business system, customer appointments, payroll and stock were on her PC. She needed it to run her four beauty salons effectively. But that PC was currently the victim of ransomware and was useless. Effectively, her business was crippled. She had no way of accessing anything.

Okay, she responded with a sigh. *How do I pay?*

Moira Haigh closed her eyes. This was a nightmare. She wanted to refuse outright, tell the blackmailer she'd go to the police, but there was no guarantee they would catch him. He was anonymous and could be running this scam from anywhere in the world. Moira had little choice but to do what she was told. But whatever he asked for, if indeed it was a he, would have to come out of her private funds, as the business just about broke even. She might have four salons dotted around the Leesworth villages, but margins were tight.

I'll text a payment link — the amount required is £50k worth of bitcoin. If you don't know what that is, or how to acquire it, do an internet search. Once I see it safely paid over, I'll release your system. Do not go to the police. They will not be able to help you. Neither these texts nor the money can be traced.

Fifty thousand pounds! Moira's heart sank. There was no way she could get her hands on that much money. She'd expected him to ask for much less. Perhaps the police were the better bet after all. They had clever technical people working for them nowadays. If she reported the scam, they might be able to stop him.

A text from Joan Radcliffe interrupted her thoughts. Gina hadn't turned up for work again and the police had been round asking for her. Moira felt sick. She knew that Gina had gone away for a few days, but could only guess at what the police wanted her for. As if she didn't have enough on her plate!

She tried to call her niece's number, but without success — the girl's phone was turned off. What trouble had she brought to the house now? Gina would never change. She was just like her mother, Marcie, a feckless druggie who did as she pleased. Just thinking of her sister and what she'd put her through because of her habit was upsetting. It had been bad enough when she'd come home pregnant at sixteen. Whoever Gina's father was had bailed as soon as he learned of Marcie's condition. Within months of Gina's birth, Marcie Haigh disappeared too. There was no way Moira could cope with a baby, and Gina was put into care. Then, when she turned sixteen, Moira had offered her a home on the understanding that she went to college and worked part-time.

Helping Gina was all very well, but Moira had to do what was best for herself now. Gina could go to hell. She didn't give a damn about what was going on in her aunt's life anyway. Moira began to grow angry. There was no way she was going to pay the blackmailer that amount of money. She'd find an IT expert to help instead. After all, she backed her system up daily, so theoretically, she should be fine.

You'll get nothing from me. Don't make contact again.

He replied, *You're dead* ☺

CHAPTER 7

Day 2

Calladine called a team briefing in the incident room. He'd just gathered the reports and notes he'd made off his desk and was about to join the others when his office phone rang. It was Superintendent Quaid.

"Good morning, sir."

"I'll get straight to the point, Calladine. I was disappointed when I got your letter. I simply don't understand why you'd refuse the DCI position on a permanent basis. But I presume that you know your own mind, so I'll respect your wishes, not that I approve of your decision. Anyway, I've solved the problem and you'll be pleased to know that I've found a new DCI for your station. He'll be joining you this morning."

Calladine smiled. This was good news, it put him firmly back on the frontline, where he belonged. "May I ask who the new DCI is, sir?"

"Stephen Greco."

The smile vanished from Calladine's face. *Greco!* Why him of all people? Was this Quaid getting his own back? No, it couldn't be, Quaid had no way of knowing that the two didn't get on.

"I expect DCI Greco to integrate quickly and that the teams in Leesdon will make him welcome."

How to answer that one? "Naturally, sir."

Call over, Calladine sat for a moment at his desk, a frown on his face. What the hell was he going to tell the team?

There was a tap on the office door. It was Ruth. "You ready, Tom? We're all waiting." She eyed him. "You look a bit grey. Bad news?"

"Quaid's been on. I'm off the hook DCI-wise but my replacement is Greco."

Ruth entered the office, closing the door behind her. "Serves you right." Much to Calladine's annoyance, she looked amused. "You can't have things all your own way, Tom. You didn't want the job and DCIs are hardly queuing up to serve in our little backwater. Greco is a good detective. Give him a chance, it'll be fine."

Calladine doubted that very much. Greco wasn't easy to get along with. "No, it won't. He's a nerd with a cleanliness fetish. I can't do with the man and his weird ways. I thought he was finished anyway. You told me he got his DC pregnant. How's he come back from that one?"

"Grace Harper gave birth to a baby boy a few months ago, and before the big event Greco married her, thus avoiding any major awkwardness with his career. Grace has taken a break and Greco is clawing his way back to form."

"If I did something like that, them upstairs wouldn't make it that easy for me. What is it with the man?"

"I wouldn't say Greco's had it easy, Tom. Think about it. We don't know if he even has feelings for Grace. I was told they had a one- night drunken fumble while they were following up on a case in Brighton. Hardly the basis for a lasting relationship."

"That makes it worse. It means the marriage is simply him covering his arse. All he really wants is to keep his job, that's plain to see."

"Never mind all that now, there's nothing we can do. The team's waiting and we've got a killer to catch."

Grabbing his paperwork, Calladine followed Ruth down the corridor to the incident briefing room. He had to get his head in order, but the news about Greco had thrown him.

Rocco, Alice and Joyce, the team's admin assistant — plus two uniformed officers — were waiting. "Right, you lot," Calladine began. "What have we got?"

Rocco went first. "Ramsey worked at the supermarket, as we know. He was well liked and had been put on the management programme. The manager, Joan Radcliffe, couldn't think of anyone who'd want to harm him. But he was pally with one Gina Haigh. She is something of an oddball. I got the impression that Radcliffe isn't keen on the girl. Gina hasn't been seen since Ramsey's murder. In fact, she disappeared just as the poisoning was taking place. I spoke to another girl working there, one Kelly Munroe. She told me that Gina had a boyfriend, Arron Cookson, known as Cooksie. The landlord of the Pheasant confirmed that on the night he was killed, Ramsey was in there watching football and getting bladdered."

"First things first, we find Gina, and bring her in for questioning. Ramsey may have confided in her," Calladine said. "Speak to the boyfriend too. Was there anything on the supermarket CCTV?"

"The film wasn't clear. A bloke wearing dark clothing with a hood over his head and down over his face. He can be seen quite clearly moving along the fridge where the drink cartons are."

"Do we know what the poison was?" Ruth asked.

"Ipecac syrup. It's an emetic, hence the throwing up. The juice in the cartons contained enough to induce light vomiting but not to do any real damage," Rocco said.

"For what purpose, I wonder?" puzzled Ruth.

"It may or may not be connected to Ramsey. We need more information before we can make a decision," Calladine said. "When we find Gina Haigh, she might be able to tell us."

"She lives with her aunt in Lowermill," Rocco said. "Apparently she left work earlier, at about the same time as the poisoning incident."

"Ruth and I will pay her a visit this morning. Alice?" Calladine looked at her.

"Ramsey lived in a children's home for most of his life. Gina Haigh was in the same home, so that's possibly where they met," Alice said.

"If she had an auntie, what was she doing in care?" Ruth asked.

"You'll have to speak to them to get the answer to that one," Rocco said. "God knows what happened to Gina's mother, and no one has any idea who her father is. Her auntie didn't take her on until six months ago. Before that, apart from the kid's home, Gina had a succession of foster home placements."

"Poor kid, she's been pushed from pillar to post. I'm not surprised she's a handful," Ruth said.

"We need more background on Ramsey," Calladine said. "It wasn't a random killing — the murderer took their time, wanted him to suffer. All of which makes it likely that the killer knew him and had a score to settle. Rocco, Alice, take a close look at Ramsey's time in that home and find out all you can."

Calladine was momentarily distracted by a figure making his way along the corridor towards the incident room. He grimaced. He knew very well who that figure was. Greco entered the room and stood at the back. He had a folder in his hands, no doubt the notes on the current case.

Greco coughed. "You appear to have everything in hand."

"DCI Greco is taking Birch's place as our new permanent DCI as of today," Calladine said with a wry smile.

Everyone's eyes turned in his direction. Greco was tall with blond cropped hair, and smartly dressed in a dark suit.

"I will spend today settling into my office and updating myself on your current cases. I would appreciate a report on your activities within the next twenty-four hours."

Calladine nodded. "Certainly, sir. We are investigating a particularly nasty murder. There isn't much in the way of forensic reports yet, but you can access them from the system as and when they arrive."

Greco walked towards the corridor. "I'd appreciate a word later, Tom."

"Him!" Rocco exclaimed as soon as Greco was out of earshot.

"Yes, him. Sorry, team. I blame myself, I've let you down. This is all my fault. We got Greco because I refused the position."

CHAPTER 8

Getting the money out of them was all well and good, but it was the ones who didn't pay that he really enjoyed. They made the enterprise so much more fun. Moira Haigh was a case in point. She was going to die, and not in a pleasant way either. The woman had refused to play ball, so she would suffer for it.

He raised a gloved hand and rapped on her front door.

The woman who answered looked him up and down with distaste. That'd be the overalls.

His smile was friendly and open. He didn't want to raise her suspicions. "Mrs Haigh? I'm Michael, the new window cleaner. I've taken over the round and wanted to introduce myself."

She sniffed disdainfully. "Windows are next week. I do hope you're not going to change the routine."

He shook his head. "No, nothing like that. I simply want you to know who we are so you feel secure when me or one of my operatives turns up at the house."

"Will they have ID?" she asked. "You can't be too careful."

"I have two young men working for me," he said. "I have a leaflet with their photos on. Come with me to the van and you can have one."

She followed him without argument. Her refusal to pay up had given him another opportunity to hone his skills and he wasn't about to miss it. He was good at this. Moira Haigh never suspected a thing. Minutes later, she lay on the floor of the van, unconscious. Taken off guard, she'd had no time to offer any resistance at all.

He'd deal with her shortly. She needed a sharp lesson in manners. Her refusal to pay up had annoyed him and he'd make sure she suffered for it. Then he would focus on the big one. His next victim was definitely all about the money, and a far more lucrative prospect than Moira Haigh, so outfoxing the police was more important than ever.

Eve Buckley was wealthy and as the major employer in this area, well known. But she was all over the place, a woman who tried to be all things to all people. Employer, wife, mother, and grandmother to a number of small children who were often left in her care. Targeting her was risky. Would she go running to that family of hers? Her son was a detective on the local force.

One way to ensure Eve did as she was told, paid the money and kept quiet was to add a threat into the mix that she couldn't ignore.

When she disappeared, there would be an outcry and many would ask questions, not least that detective son of hers. But he'd deal with that, and the rewards would be worth it.

He'd done his research. The pub nearest to the factory was full of Buckley's staff after work and they were only too happy to gossip. Wednesday was her working day. Each Wednesday she went to Buckley Pharmaceuticals to ensure that all was progressing as it should. Her son, Simon, supposedly held the reins, but Eve couldn't relinquish control. The attack on their IT system would happen on her watch. Eve Buckley would panic, blame herself and then demand that the problem be fixed. Once she realised it was impossible, she'd do as he told her and agree to his terms.

It would begin as it always did, with an email. Eve could be disorganised, but she wasn't stupid. She would be well versed on suspicious attachments. So, it had to look convincing.

* * *

Rocco and Alice had followed every lead in an effort to find Gina Haigh, but to no effect. Her friends had no idea where she might have gone and her aunt wasn't answering the phone, so that was a dead end too. But Arron Cookson was another matter.

They found him hanging around the entrance to Heron House. The two detectives parked up and watched him.

"Kids on bikes — look." Alice pointed. "Every few seconds another one pulls up and Arron hands something over."

"Drugs, I bet. He's dealing and he's not afraid to do so in broad daylight. The idiot deserves everything that's coming to him."

"It's not casual dealing though, is it? He's organised. We've been watching for fifteen minutes and the stream of kids is constant. We should ask ourselves who's supplying him," Alice said.

They approached slowly, keeping a wary eye on Cookson. They didn't want to spook him. The lad was tall and lean, wiry, and if he got wind that they were police, he'd be off like a shot and they'd have a devil of a job catching him again.

Not until they were within a few metres of him did Alice smile and ask, "Arron Cookson?"

He backed up against the wall of the tower block. "Who wants to know?"

"We're police, Arron," Rocco said. "We want to talk to Gina, your girlfriend. Do you know where she is?"

That seemed to relax him. "Ask her auntie, or at the supermarket where she works. I haven't seen her in days."

"We've done that but had no luck," said Alice. "C'mon, Arron, you can do better than that. Where is she? Why doesn't she want to show herself?"

"No idea. I'm not her keeper. Gina does as she pleases."

A kid on a bike flew past the group, grinned widely and then spat at Rocco, missing him by inches. "Nice company you keep," the detective said. "We're getting nowhere out here. I think we'd better continue this down at the station."

"And if I don't want to come with you?"

"Given what's in your pocket, I don't think you have much choice. We've been watching you for a while from over there, and we've seen you openly dealing to those kids. That can get you into serious trouble," Rocco said.

"About time you changed your tune and helped us, Arron," Alice added. "That way things might go better for you."

CHAPTER 9

Once they were alone and on their way to Lowermill, Ruth said, "The team aren't happy."

She was stating the obvious. Calladine had seen their faces. "They're not alone, and I meant it when I said I blame myself. All I had to do was take the bloody job."

"It would have killed you, Tom. You're not a desk detective and you know it. It might suit the likes of Birch, but not you."

"How d'you imagine Greco will cope?"

"I doubt he had much choice. It'll have been Leesdon or retirement, and he's only in his thirties." She nudged his arm. "Think about it. He had an affair with a junior member of his team, got her pregnant. Given the circumstances, Stephen Greco had to do what he was told."

Ruth was right, but it didn't help, they were still saddled with the man. Calladine's mobile rang. It was his mother, Eve Buckley.

"Eve," he said. "You okay?"

Eve was the owner of Buckley Pharmaceuticals, the firm she'd inherited from her husband. Eve and Calladine had only met recently, after the woman he'd always thought was his biological mother, had died. It turned out that Tom

Calladine was the result of a relationship his father had had with Eve. She'd been young, unable to cope with a newborn, so Frank Calladine took in the infant, and he and his wife, Jean, had raised him. Calladine had found it difficult to cope with the truth of his parentage. He'd loved Jean, and she'd raised him as her own. The fact of this stranger, the woman with the big house and the company that employed half of Leesworth, being his mother, was taking some getting used to.

"I could do with a word, Tom. We're having a birthday party next week for my grandson, Mark, Simon's eldest son. He's eighteen and I'd like you to come. Bring someone, if you want. I believe Amy is back in Leesdon."

Eve on her own was just about okay but throw in the rest of them and Calladine felt way out of his depth.

"I'll see. We have a lot on at work just now," he said.

"Try your best, we'd all like you to be there."

He heard the disappointment in her voice and felt guilty. He should try harder — people were always telling him that. Like it or not, Eve was his mother. She had other children besides Calladine, yet she was trying hard to build a relationship with him.

"How's Zoe? Is the baby doing okay?"

"Yep, all's fine on that score. I'll show you a scan picture when I see you."

Once the call was over, Ruth said, "You've not mentioned Eve recently."

"I don't get the time for chatty little visits, and to be honest, I find her and the others, my half siblings, daunting. That's one huge house Eve lives in, and one or other of them is always in the local paper for one reason or another."

"The Buckleys are like royalty round here, you know that."

"That'll be the reason I don't fit in, I'm far too ordinary, plus I mostly mix with lowlife."

Ruth nudged him. "Stop feeling sorry for yourself. And I hope you're not referring to me when you say *lowlife*. Pull up over there, we've arrived." She pointed. "Rocco and Alice rang Moira Haigh earlier and got no response. The car is in the drive, so we might have more luck."

The house was a detached newbuild on a small estate above the village of Lowermill. It had a neat front garden, a small lawn bordered by flower beds and a high privet hedge.

A woman called to them from across the road. "Moira's not here."

"D'you know where she's gone? She's not taken her car. Did you see her leave?" Ruth asked.

"No. I've been across and rung the bell several times but got no answer."

"D'you have any idea where she might be, or when she'll be back?" asked Calladine.

"Are you the police?"

Ruth showed the woman her badge. "Yes. Who are you?"

"Pat Eccles, I live across the road. I'm a bit concerned about Moira. I heard people talking out here earlier. I took a peek through the blinds, but I couldn't see what was going on. There was a vehicle though, parked on the drive behind her car. It must have been there about ten minutes, and then it disappeared. I came across to see if Moira was okay, but I couldn't raise her."

"Did you see Moira get into the vehicle?" Ruth asked.

"No, there's a high hedge and that tree on the grass verge blocks the view."

"You said 'vehicle,' not car, couldn't you be sure?"

"No, I couldn't. Like I said, the view is obstructed and I didn't have my glasses on."

"Do you have a key to the house, or know where we might get one?"

After a moment's thought, she said, "Mrs Roper next door, she might have one."

Calladine nodded at Ruth. "Thanks. We'll find out what's going on."

Ruth went next door and returned with a woman in tow. "Mrs Roper, and the key to Moira Haigh's house."

"C'mon then, let's take a look." Calladine turned to the two women. "Stay out here, if you would, back there on the pavement."

"You look worried," Ruth said.

"Her niece is missing, a workmate of said niece is dead. I'm keeping an open mind until we've been inside."

But the inside of Moira Haigh's home yielded nothing. Moira wasn't home and, like Ramsey's place, it was as neat as a new pin. Ruth went upstairs and took a look around.

"Beds made, nothing out of place up there," she said, joining him downstairs. "The place looks as if she's just nipped out for a few minutes."

"She didn't take her car and the shops are some distance away. She's not in the immediate area, the neighbours would know. I think Moira Haigh got into that vehicle."

"Don't be melodramatic. It might have been a friend picking her up, or perhaps she's gone to stay with a relative," Ruth said.

Calladine looked at her and shook his head. "I don't like this. Get onto Julian, or that Rob you're so fond of, ask them to send a team over to take a proper look round."

CHAPTER 10

"Hello, Ruth, it's Rob. I thought you should know. Remember those flecks of dark blue paint we found on Kieron Ramsey's clothing? Further analysis showed it to be automobile paint. I can probably give you the make and model, but that will take a little longer."

Ruth was back in the incident room when she took the call. "Thanks, Rob, that's useful info. Anything else?"

"The paint had rust particles on it. If I had to guess I'd say the vehicle was old."

"You think Ramsey met his end in this vehicle?"

"Given there was no blood where he was found, that is a strong possibility. My people have searched the area extensively and found nothing. I can only conclude that Ramsey was killed either inside a building or a van and transported to the dump site."

What he said made sense. "A van, you say. He lived on the Hobfield. He'd spent the evening in the Pheasant pub, so he didn't have far to get home. He'd walk, the killer must have approached him then. If he was killed in the back of a van, he could simply have been thrown out once the killer had finished with him."

"Until we have concrete proof, that is simply conjecture," Rob said.

Ruth was hanging on his every word. Not because of what he had to say, but because she enjoyed listening to him. She found herself wishing that he'd just keep talking, it didn't matter what about. She shook herself. What was happening? There was no way she could fall for this man and anyway, like Calladine had reminded her, she had Jake. Ruth Bayliss had known Rob Harris was dangerous the moment she'd set eyes on him. She might have a problem with Jake, but their son, Harry, was a different matter. She had to get a grip.

"Keep us posted with anything else you find, Rob," Ruth said.

Rocco joined her. "We've brought Arron Cookson in," he said. "The villain was openly dealing outside Heron House. He's been searched and we found about two thousand pounds' worth of crack on him."

"That's not what we want him for though, is it? Does he know anything about Gina Haigh?"

Rocco rolled his eyes. "He says not, but he's a lying toe-rag who couldn't tell the truth if his life depended on it."

Ruth accessed Rob's report off the system, printed it out and handed it to Rocco. "Looks like we're looking for a dark blue van. Forensics reckon Ramsey was inside one before he died."

"What about Arron Cookson?" Rocco asked.

"We'll have to charge him with possession and dealing. Look at his background. He might be young, but I bet he's got a record. Have we checked?"

"I'll find out. Where's the boss?" Rocco asked.

"Which one?"

"Calladine, of course. I don't think I'll ever get used to Greco."

"He's not bad. Try giving him a chance, Rocco. After all, we're going to have to work with the man, like it or not."

* * *

Calladine had been summoned to Greco's office. The man had only been with them half a day, but he'd already cleared the place out and had it cleaned. Calladine hadn't bothered, he'd simply found a space amongst Birch's clutter. This was an aspect of Greco's personality he could not get used to.

Greco gestured for Calladine to sit down. "Until DI Long returns to work, us two and the teams will have to make this work. As has been usual with the DCI at this station, my role will be mostly background. Essentially, I've become a desk detective, which doesn't suit me at all."

Calladine understood that. It hadn't suited him either. "Didn't they give you a choice?"

"No, and I don't blame them. To be honest, Tom, I expected to be booted out after what happened with Grace. In many respects, I'm lucky."

Calladine smiled. He didn't think it was lucky — a desk job would've killed him. "You have my sympathies, sir."

"Please, call me Stephen. I want us to be friends, Tom. I'm going to need all the help I can get. There's no sign of Brad Long returning after his heart attack. I will oversee his team and leave you to sort yours. But any problems, please shout. This new case you're investigating, how's it going?"

"We've got a body and that's about all. I believe some forensics have come in this morning which might help. But the victim hasn't made it easy. He was a hardworking soul with no record, little money and led a blameless life. We can't find anything to work with."

"He upset someone, knew something, saw something. From what little I know of the Hobfield, it's not hard to fall foul of villains. You need to dig deeper."

About to utter some quip about stating the obvious, Calladine bit it back. After all, Greco had offered the hand of friendship and although he didn't much like the new DCI, for the sake of the team he had to try his best to at least meet him halfway.

"We are looking at friends and colleagues. Interestingly, one of them has done a runner. We've brought someone in this morning who might give us a lead."

"Good, we all need this tied up quickly."

"We'll do our best, Stephen. I can't say fairer than that."

As Calladine returned to the incident room, an excited Rocco called out. "Alice has done some digging, and guess what? Cookson owns an old, dark blue transit. Fits the spec a treat, I'd say."

"Arron Cookson, the young man in the cells? He's Gina Haigh's boyfriend. Find that van and get forensics on it," Calladine ordered. "I think we need a serious word with young Cookson."

"Do you think the connection between Ramsey and Cookson is Gina?" Alice asked. "The motive could be jealousy, don't you think?"

"Possibly."

"Gina and Ramsey knew each other from work. Perhaps they got close and Cookson didn't like it."

CHAPTER 11

Lonely, surrounded by trees and sheltered by the steep slopes of the Pennine Hills, Doveclough Lake was small, as lakes go. Built to serve as an overflow for the much larger reservoir in the hills above, it was nonetheless known to be deep and dangerous. It was also well off the beaten track. The walkers that clambered over this terrain tended to keep to the paths that took them over the tops and on towards the Yorkshire villages.

There was a track of sorts, narrow and pitted, but with care a four-wheel drive vehicle could navigate it and wouldn't be seen from the paths below.

There was a killing from the past that he wanted the police to connect to this one. Nonetheless, it was the perfect spot to bring Moira Haigh's body. A quiet and peaceful place used by fishermen and ramblers. Naked, wrapped in fabric, taped up tight and weighted with just enough stones so that the body would sink. But it would be found. One day soon, despite the stones, the body would bloat and rise to the surface.

This was not down to him. It was her own fault. Moira Haigh did not need to die. If she'd paid up, he would have given her back her system and she wouldn't have heard from him again. But it was too late now. In the final stages of the ordeal, he'd made her suffer. She'd begged him to let her go.

She'd known what was coming, seen the knife in his hand, felt it cut into her body even before it touched her skin. In the end, bleeding heavily, battered and with blackened, swollen eyes, she stared at the blade he wielded in front of her face and lost her mind. Killing her had been a kindness. There was no way she could return to normal life. Moira Haigh was too damaged by then.

* * *

Calladine returned to his office. He wanted to speak to Julian, if he was on duty. Ruth might reckon Rob was okay, but things were moving too slowly for him.

He was surprised to see Superintendent Quaid waiting for him.

"Your team are busy."

"We've got a killer to find, we won't do that sitting around, sir."

"I've got another appointment, so I won't keep you. Walk with me to my car."

Quaid made his way out into the corridor and down the stairs. He was in thoughtful mode — that wasn't good. Calladine had no idea what this was about, there had been no warning of his visit.

"Greco settling, is he?" Quaid asked.

"Made himself at home, up to speed with the case, so, yes, I'd say so, sir. Is that why you want a word? Is this about Greco?"

"No, something far more serious, I'm afraid. Clifford Machin is out." Quaid fell silent for a few seconds, letting the news sink in. "He was released three months ago, but no one thought to let us know. He is on licence and as far as I'm aware, he's sticking to the conditions."

Calladine inhaled sharply. This wasn't good news. Clifford Machin was an old enemy, who at one time had worked closely with two other villains — Calladine's cousin Ray Fallon and Reggie York.

"Where's he living?"

"Better you don't know. You need to keep well away."

"He knows where to find me," Calladine argued.

"You put him away, Calladine, and he has resented you for it ever since. I haven't forgotten the threats he made against you at his trial. But apparently, he's been the perfect inmate. During his time inside he hasn't put a foot wrong and was considered a good risk for release."

"They were bloody wrong on that one, sir," Calladine blurted out. Machin was a piece of work, and he'd hoped never to hear his name again. "I'm surprised he was released so soon. He never told anyone what he did with the body of that young man, despite the family's pleas."

"Because he's always maintained his innocence," Quaid said. "He says we got the wrong man. Reckons it was Ray Fallon who killed that lad, and that Fallon alone knew what had happened to the body."

"I'm not sticking up for him. As you know, me and Fallon have history, some of it personal. Fallon is dead now, but he was interviewed as I recall, and he provided an alibi we couldn't fault."

Quaid sighed. "Well, the bloke who stood in Fallon's corner has since died, and as you said, so has Fallon. Reggie York has vanished from the picture, so I suppose we'll never know for sure."

"I'll have to watch my step. Machin might have kept his nose clean inside, but there have been rumours over the years," Calladine said. "I know he wants me dead. That outburst at his sentencing, the threats he made against me and mine still give me sleepless nights. He blames me for having him put away, and for Fallon's death."

"We can't be sure, but he could have you in his sights," Quaid said. "Do you want protection?"

"No, sir, I'll manage if it's all the same." The last thing Calladine wanted was having a couple of uniforms shadow him. "Has he made any concrete threats?"

"No, but that's not his style, is it?"

CHAPTER 12

Arron Cookson was agitated, his thin face was flushed and he couldn't sit still. He kept shifting in his seat and glancing up at the clock on the wall.

"Got somewhere to be, Arron? Or perhaps you're missing your fix?" Calladine asked. "I'm guessing you're every bit as addicted to that rubbish you peddle as those you supply."

"You've got it wrong, Copper. I'm not an addict and I don't supply either. That other bloke, he took my phone. I want it back. I need it for my business."

"I bet you do," Calladine said. "We're checking it out, to get what information we can from it."

Cookson grinned. "It's a pay-as-you-go, there's no contract."

"You still need a provider," Calladine said. "They'll give us what we need."

Cookson sat back on his chair, sullen.

"You had a small fortune in crack on you when you were arrested. How d'you explain that?" Calladine went on.

Cookson shrugged and looked away.

"C'mon, this is your chance to explain. Tell us where it came from, Arron, or suffer the consequences."

"I found it, dumped in a bin on the estate. I knew what it was and thought I'd make a bob or two. It was a mistake, that's all."

"That's a load of rubbish, an insult to our intelligence. Who are you working for?" Calladine said.

"No one. I told you, I found it."

"Tell us the truth, Arron, or you won't like the consequences."

"I can't. I speak to you and you know what happens."

He was being threatened. Cookson didn't look the type. "Carry on the way you are and how long d'you think you'll last, eh? You're selling dope and you're an addict. Face it, Arron, you're a mess," Calladine said. "Speak to us and we'll help you sort yourself out."

"It was a mistake. I should have said no. Gina said I was bloody stupid for going along with it." He turned back to Calladine and for the first time looked him in the eye. "But you've no idea what it's like on the Hobfield. Don't do as you're told and you're dead. I might be daft, but I don't want that."

Calladine regarded him. He looked every bit the street-wise budding villain, but was that all show? Calladine wanted to know more. "Pull the other one, Arron. This is down to you alone. You started this, no one else. We haven't had many drug-related problems on the Hobfield recently. Minimal dealing, a few teens caught with weed, nothing serious, and now you're telling us we're wrong. Where did the drugs come from? Who's your contact?"

"It's you that's got it wrong. Dealing *is* happening and, believe me, a lot of it. Anyone with a pulse has been roped in. It isn't down to me, either, I'm just one of the idiots selling the stuff."

"Okay, tell us who is behind it. Who's the person you're afraid of, Arron?"

"I'm no grass," he sneered. "Besides, I'd like to stay in one piece, if it's all the same to you."

"It's only a matter of time before we find out. We do that in the next couple of days and bring someone in, you'll be labelled a grass anyway. You might as well come clean and we'll protect you."

"No way. No one crosses the new boss and gets off lightly. I'm not taking the risk."

So, there was a new boss. Calladine wanted more information, a name, for starters. "Okay, let's see if a few hours behind bars will convince you to speak to us."

There was a knock on the interview door. It was Rocco, beckoning to him. Calladine went outside.

"Uniform has found a burnt-out van on a patch of spare land off the Huddersfield Road. That road goes over the tops and the place where the van was found isn't easy to see. Forensics are looking at it, and Dr Harris is running tests. He reckons it could be the blue transit we're looking for. What's the betting it turns out to be Cookson's?"

"Good work."

Calladine went back inside and sat down opposite Cookson and the duty solicitor. "You own an old van. Where do you keep it?"

"What's my van got to do with this?"

"Just answer the question."

"It should be parked up at the side of the towers, not that it's any business of yours."

"When did you use it last?" Calladine asked.

"Can't remember. It breaks down a lot so I don't drive it much."

"When, Arron?" Calladine said.

"Last week. I took Gina into Oldston to do a bit of shopping."

Calladine nodded. "Do you know a Kieron Ramsey?"

Cookson looked puzzled. "Yeah, he's the idiot who's been stalking Gina. Works at hers and follows her all over the place."

"That must bother her. Bother you too, does it?"

"He's a joke. Gina makes fun of him. Anyway, he doesn't stand a chance. Gina would never go with the likes of him."

"When did you last see Kieron?" Calladine asked.

"I don't know, not for a day or so. But he does that, drops off the radar. He'll be back."

Calladine studied the young man in front of him. Was he telling the truth? He'd spoken of Kieron Ramsey without so much as a flicker of guilt.

"Can I go now?" Cookson asked.

"No, Arron. First we have the problem of the drugs, and then there's Kieron."

"What about him?"

"He's been murdered, and currently, Arron, you are our prime suspect."

It took a moment for the words to sink in. Cookson's eyes widened in horror and he started to shake. "I've not killed anybody!" he shouted. "You've got this all wrong, copper. Why would I kill Kieron? I don't even know him that well."

"You know who he is, and you've just told me he's been stalking your girlfriend. I'd say you'd got his measure, alright. Where were you Sunday night?"

"I . . . I'm not sure. I can't think." He paused for a moment, his eyes all over the place. He looked at his solicitor, who was taking notes, and then scoured the walls for inspiration. "I think that was the night me and G got bladdered. We were in a pub in Hopecross. Not our usual place, but Gina fancied a change. That was the night County won at home, we walked back to Leesdon with some fish and chips to celebrate. There were others with us, ask them."

Calladine passed Cookson a pen and paper. "Write down exactly where you went and as many names as you can recall. We need to talk to every last one of them."

Cookson looked up, twitchy again. "You're going to bother my mates. I'll be lucky not to get a beating."

"Why Hopecross? That isn't your usual haunt. The Pheasant is more your mark."

"G wanted to try out that new place, the pub in the square. There's no mystery about it."

Calladine didn't believe him for a moment. There would have been a reason behind the visit to Hopecross, but right now he was more concerned about the murder. "Do you keep your van locked up, Arron?"

The lad hesitated. "Yeah, course, but it's old, one good pull on the door handle and it's open."

"Does anyone else use it?"

"I don't know. I doubt it. My van's old, battered. Most folk wouldn't be seen dead in a heap like that."

Calladine gathered up his papers and made to leave. "You'll be spending a little longer with us, Arron."

"But it's late. I need to get home."

"Don't worry, we'll make you comfortable. And we'll speak again tomorrow. By the way, do you know where Gina is?"

Cookson shrugged. "I'm not her keeper. If she's not at work, I've no idea."

Again, he looked shifty. Calladine would speak to him again when he'd had time to think things through. Interview over, he left the room and told the uniformed officer with him to take the lad to the cells.

Back in the incident room, Ruth was packing up for the day. "It's getting late, I'll have to go. Jake will be wondering what's happened to me."

"No probs, you get off. See you tomorrow."

CHAPTER 13

Before he left for the day, Calladine checked the messages on his mobile. Both Eve and Zoe wanted to see him. He sighed. It was getting late and all he wanted was a night in front of his fire with a glass of whisky. But he couldn't ignore them both. He decided that seeing Zoe was more important. He'd ring Eve and put her off until tomorrow.

It wasn't far from Leesdon to the village of Lowermill, where his daughter lived with her partner, Jo Brandon. The pair had recently bought a small cottage by the canal that ran along the back of the High Street, and were still settling in.

Zoe greeted him with a kiss on the cheek. "You saw the scan pic? Great, isn't it? Everything is fine with the baby. I've told Julian to relax, but he's still stressing. To be honest, Dad, he's doing my head in. I was in that hospital waiting room today with Jo, Julian, and Amy — I know I invited Julian, but Amy's a bit much. They kept going on about diet and booze. You'd think I was a kid, not a grown woman."

"Julian's never done this before. He just wants what's best, he's looking out for you."

"Me and Jo have never done this before either. I don't want to cut them out of things completely, but Julian can't seem to stop worrying. Speak to Amy and get her to have a word with him. He rings me at least three times a day and it's beyond a joke."

Calladine nodded. He'd try but he doubted he'd have much luck. "The place is coming on." He went over to the French doors. "The garden's looking nice."

"That's down to Jo. Turns out she has green fingers. On summer nights we'll be able to sit down there and watch the ducks on the canal."

"You'll have to keep the little one away once it starts to move, put up a fence or something. That canal can get deep when it rains."

"We will. You're beginning to sound exactly like the rest of them. Me and Jo do know what we're doing."

"When you're ready, give us a shout and I'll come round and do it for you," he said.

Zoe ignored the offer. "Has Eve been in touch?"

"About Mark's birthday, yes. I'll try to show my face but I can't promise."

"Me neither. I've never met the lad," Zoe said, "and I see precious little of Simon, so me and Jo will probably give it a miss. Eve's another one — she wants to organise a 'baby shower.' Give them a chance, and the relatives will take over this pregnancy completely."

"Eve's your grandmother. You know the history, she's got a lot of making up to do. She means well."

"I'm sorry but I can't help thinking of Jean in that role. She'd have been perfect."

Calladine felt uncomfortable comparing Eve and Jean in this way. He still had mixed emotions about his past and what had been kept from him. "Is this what you wanted me for, family stuff?"

"Partly, but there is something else, possibly important, possibly not. Our business on the High Street is next door to a beauty salon, one of those owned by Moira Haigh."

Now she had his full attention. "Do you know the woman?" he asked.

59

"No, but the manager of the salon, Dorothy Ainscough, knows that my dad is a detective," she smiled, "and she asked me to have a word. Dorothy thinks something has happened to Moira. She has nothing concrete to go on, but Moira isn't answering her mobile or house phone, she hasn't responded to emails or processed the payroll this month. We all got a text to say not to come in as the computer system in her office wasn't working and she couldn't access anything. She was going to get it fixed and tell them when to return. Dorothy tried contacting her, but with no luck. She has a set of keys and went to Moira's salon. She was right, the booking system and everything else was locked up. She asked her husband about it, he works in IT, and he said the way Dorothy described it, it sounded like ransomware."

"Moira Haigh is connected to a current case of ours," Calladine said soberly. "There's probably a simple explanation, so don't worry. I'll look into it."

* * *

Ruth had texted Jake earlier in the afternoon to let him know that she'd be late. The instructions were to take the casserole she'd made at the weekend out of the freezer and stick it in the oven. But as she entered the hallway of their home, there was no smell of cooking.

She was annoyed. The task was simple enough. "Jake!" she called. But there was no reply. The house was empty, there was no sign of Jake or their son. It didn't look as if he'd been home at all. The breakfast pots were still in the sink and Harry's pyjamas were still on the sofa, where he'd thrown them this morning. A quick check in the shed showed Jake's bike wasn't there either. These days he pedalled to Leesworth Academy, where he worked.

Panic! If Jake hadn't collected Harry, where the hell was their son? Not at nursery, that closed two hours ago.

"Ruth," a woman called from the hallway. "It's Anna from across the road. I hope you don't mind — the front door was open. I've brought Harry home."

Ruth felt a surge of relief. But what was Jake playing at?

"Jake rang me and asked if I'd pick the little lad up from nursery," Anna explained. "He's a bit muddy, I'm afraid, we've been playing football in the park."

Ruth rushed forward and hugged her son. "Thanks, Anna, you're a lifesaver. Jake was supposed to fetch him today. I'd no idea he'd asked you to step in. If I had, I'd have come home sooner."

"It was no problem, I'm at home all day and Harry's such a good little boy. I picked him up at three, gave him his tea and then we went to the park."

"Did Jake say why he'd be late?"

"No, just that something had come up."

That was unusual. School meetings were marked on the calendar, so that the two of them could work around them. It was rare that anything happened out of the blue that stopped Jake coming home on time. Her job was erratic, they both accepted that, but Jake's was routine and ran according to a strict timetable.

Once Anna had left, Ruth rang Jake on his mobile. It went straight to voicemail. That usually meant he was in a meeting at school, but it was seven-thirty. Suddenly a message flashed on the screen. It was him.

Sorry, I'll explain when I get back, home in ten.

Nothing about what had kept him, and why hadn't Jake texted her this afternoon if he was going to be late?

CHAPTER 14

Day 3

The following morning all the team, apart from Ruth, gathered in the incident room for a briefing. Ruth had rung in earlier to say she'd be late. She gave no explanation and Calladine had detected an edge in her tone. He was concerned, but he had Greco breathing down his neck for a result, so he decided to shelve speaking to her for later.

He took a quick look through the reports. The only new forensic information that had come in was that both Kieron Ramsey and Moira Haigh's homes had yielded nothing untoward. What he really wanted was the burnt-out van to give them something they could use. Before speaking to the team, he had dropped Rob Harris an email. He needed results, and quick.

"Do we have anything new?" he began. "Rocco?"

"According to Cookson's statement," the DC began, "there is plenty of dealing happening on the Hobfield, so I decided to take a look for myself."

Calladine raised an eyebrow. "You went on your own?"

Rocco nodded.

"Don't do that again. You know perfectly well how dangerous the Hobfield is. I do not want you taking any undue risks. What would have happened if you'd been recognised?"

"I wasn't, sir, and I didn't take any risks. It was dark. I parked between the two towers, sat in my car, lights off, and watched."

Calladine nodded but wasn't happy. Rocco had been injured by villains on that estate in the past.

"I didn't have to wait long," Rocco continued. "Cookson was right about the dealing but he didn't tell us the important bit, like just how involved he is. There's a flat on the ground floor of Heron House and I saw upwards of twenty or more youngsters visit. Most were on push bikes. They entered the flat and left minutes later."

"Do you know who rents that flat?"

Rocco smiled. "Arron Cookson himself."

"In that case, our Mr Cookson has some explaining to do. He must have quite a set-up for it to continue while he's locked up," said Calladine.

"I doubt it's down to Cookson alone. In my opinion he's not that bright," Rocco said.

"Any idea who he's working with? Did you spot any likely contenders?"

"After about an hour, things quietened down, and I took a ride round. There was a smart-looking sports car parked on the rough ground near where we found Ramsey. I checked the registration on the database this morning. It's owned by one Noah Ash," Rocco said.

That was not a name Calladine recognised. But in the ever-changing micro world that was the Hobfield, that wasn't unusual. "Good work, Rocco, we'll have a word with him. Where does he live?"

Rocco cleared his throat nervously. "He lives with his parents. The Ash family are Eve Buckley's neighbours."

"I see." Calladine nodded. "Noah Ash's family has money. Okay, you and I will take a drive up there and have a word. Let's hope he's got a good reason for being on the Hobfield last night."

Calladine looked at Alice. "It's possible that Moira Haigh's business computer was targeted by ransomware. Arrange for it to be brought in and then liaise with the tech boys. Keep me posted on what they find."

* * *

Ruth Bayliss sat in front of her dressing table mirror trying to cover up the ravages of a night spent weeping, but it wasn't working. Her eyes were still red and swollen, and she looked pale and drawn from loss of sleep.

Jake had arrived home, dropped his bombshell, packed an overnight bag and left. Ruth was totally unprepared. There had been no warning, nor had she spotted any signs. What he told her was devastating. By the time they'd finished arguing, sleep was out of the question. Instead, she'd spent the night pacing the sitting room floor, drinking coffee and trying to make sense of it. Even in daylight, she still didn't really believe what had happened.

Jake had another woman, a colleague from work, and he'd been seeing her for a while. Orla Gray had been in post as an English teacher in his department at Leesworth Academy since last September. They'd met up several times since, at a pub out of the area, and had even managed a week-end away last month. Ruth had been so wrapped up in her job that she couldn't even recall which weekend that was. In short, she hadn't had a clue. Jake told her it was when he was supposed to be on a trip to Haworth with the sixth formers. In fact, he'd ditched that in favour of an intimate weekend in a hotel with Orla.

Jake couldn't apologise enough. He said he'd never intended it to get this far. He had tried to end it with Orla numerous times, but it was no use, he was in love with her.

Those words cut deep, and Ruth felt the tears well up again as they echoed in her head. The pair had their problems, they argued a lot, didn't see eye to eye on many things, but Ruth believed their son Harry bound them together. How wrong she'd been.

Ruth had no idea how she was going to explain this to Harry. He wasn't yet two and couldn't possibly understand. All he'd see was that his daddy wasn't here. That was another thing. Jake had promised that his new relationship would not impinge on his duties as a father, but she was sure it would.

And then there was the team at work. What was she going to tell them? They'd be sympathetic, but they all had a job to do and personal matters took a back seat. They'd make all the right noises, but they wouldn't really understand.

Ruth took one last look in the mirror — far from perfect but she'd have to do. She sent a quick text to Anna across the road, who'd kindly taken Harry to nursery that morning and would pick him up again later. Ruth had idea no what she'd do in the long term.

CHAPTER 15

Calladine pointed out a large detached house hugging the hillside above Leesdon. "That must be it over there. That huge pile to the right is where Eve lives." He gestured to a pull-in out of sight of the houses. "Park there, behind those trees. If Eve's in I don't want her to spot me. She'll want to talk about Zoe, and that's tricky at the moment."

They parked and walked up the drive towards the Ash family's front door.

"Do you know anything about ransomware?" Calladine asked. "Moira Haigh's business system was targeted, according to an employee."

"I believe the only way to solve it is to pay up. The perpetrator locks down the system, and a key is required to free it again," Rocco said. "Sometimes they wipe the files anyway, even if you pay."

"Tricky, particularly if you can't afford it."

"Is that why she's missing, sir?"

"My instincts tell me it's connected. What do we know about this young man?" he asked.

"According to our information, Noah Ash is twenty-three, lives with his parents and is an only child. Looking at the house, I'd say the family were well-heeled enough, so what is he doing dealing drugs on the Hobfield?" Rocco asked.

"That could be where the money comes from. We'll reserve judgement until we've spoken to him. Do we know anything else?"

"There's nothing on the system," Rocco said.

A middle-aged woman answered the front door with a much younger woman hovering in her wake.

Calladine smiled at them. "We'd like to speak to Noah."

The woman, who they guessed to be Noah's mother, glanced nervously behind her. "He is not in."

"Not here," the younger woman echoed.

She sounded foreign — Polish, Calladine guessed. "Are you family?"

She shook her head. "I'm a friend."

Calladine showed her his badge. "Would you please check that Noah isn't in? We're police."

The young woman's face flushed, and she looked at Noah's mother as if to warn her of something. "I will check."

She scurried off down the corridor.

"When do you expect him back?" Rocco asked.

But before Noah's mother could speak, the younger woman was back. "He is not here. I checked his room."

"Have you come about his car?" the mother asked.

"In a way," Rocco said.

"Only he's gone to pick it up. Your people found it earlier this morning. Noah reported it missing last night. We had guests and there was no room on the drive, so he'd left it parked on the lane. When he went to move it, it had gone."

"When did he report it stolen?" Calladine asked.

"The moment he realised it was missing. That car was a birthday present from me and his father. It cost a fortune."

"Was Noah at home last night?"

"No, he was back about ten. He's a grown man," she said disdainfully. "He's free to come and go as he pleases."

"Do you know where he went?" Calladine asked.

Now she looked really annoyed. "I'm not in the habit of keeping tabs on him. What is this? What do you think my son has done?"

"We simply want him to help with enquiries, answer one or two questions." Smiling, Calladine handed her his card. "Tell him we called and ask him to come into Leesdon station for a word."

As they walked back to their car, Rocco looked back at the impressive house. "That girl with Mrs Ash, she's looking at us from an upstairs window."

"She didn't like us much, that's for sure, particularly when we asked for Noah. See if you can find out more about her when we get back."

"You think there's something going on?" Rocco asked.

"I get that feeling. If you were spotted last night, despite your best efforts, arranging to have the vehicle stolen is a get-out. Check the details, where it was found and who by."

* * *

Buckley Pharmaceuticals had been one of Leesworth's largest employers for years, and thanks to careful management was still going strong. Eve Buckley, the founder's widow, was proud of what her husband and family had built. They had succeeded in creating a workplace whose staff were happy and fulfilled.

Over the last few years, Eve had backed off, leaving her son, Simon, in charge. But she couldn't let go completely. Most Wednesdays she did a stint in the office to ensure that everything was in order and give Simon a few hours off.

Usually, the day wasn't particularly stressful. Eve checked orders, took a walk around the labs and factory and then saw to the emails. She hadn't anticipated that this Wednesday would be any different. But she was wrong.

Wendy, the new office junior, hadn't stopped chattering all morning, mostly about her college course and a boy she had her eye on. "My tutor wants to come and visit. Will that be okay?"

"Yes, just let me know the date and I'll make sure I'm here," Eve said. For the last half-hour, her attention had been split between the brimming inbox and trying to listen to what the girl was saying.

Wendy looked over her shoulder. "Most of that lot is junk," she said. "Stuff like that wastes a whole lot of time."

But some of the emails were important and needed Eve's attention. She spotted one from a customer with an amended order attached. "Have Haywards rung us with this?" she asked.

"I haven't spoken to them. Perhaps Mr Buckley did," Wendy said.

Perhaps Simon had planned to sort it, but he hadn't, and the original order had been placed a month ago. Depending on what they wanted, it could be too late to change anything now. Production would be well advanced. "I'll take a look and try to work out what we can do," said Eve.

Haywards were a regular buyer, and Eve didn't want to disappoint them. She opened the email and read through the text briefly. It looked like dozens of other emails they'd received from Haywards in the past. She clicked on the link to open the PDF document containing the new order.

With that one click, the cursor froze, and the screen filled with a paragraph of information, a padlocked chain and a notice reading, *Pay up or else*. Eve was stunned. Her stomach churned as she tried to work out what had happened. She heard Wendy gasp and Eve saw that her PC showed the same message. Eve ran out into the corridor to be met by a number of the admin staff.

"It's all of them," Alan, an accounts assistant, told her. "The entire general office has been locked down. I'll check the labs and production."

Eve returned to her office and tapped furiously on her keyboard. Nothing. She knew then what this was. Another firm they dealt with in Manchester had been hit the same way about three months ago.

Buckley Pharmaceuticals had been targeted by ransomware and she'd fallen into the trap. Why hadn't the anti-virus software kicked in? There was no time to debate this now. In a panic, Eve picked up the phone. She needed the help of an IT expert, and quickly.

"Colin," she said, her voice shaky. "It's Eve. We've got one huge problem. The office PCs have all gone down. Our system's been got at by ransomware. Can you help?"

Colin was a young man who worked for a large software company in Manchester. He had a degree in software engineering and had built the original system Buckley's used.

Alan popped his head around her office door. "The labs and factory PCs are all okay," he said.

"Did you hear that? It's just the office," she said.

"It still doesn't sound good, Eve. This will be followed by a demand for money, most likely to be paid in bitcoin. Turn everything off and I'll get a team round pronto, but to be honest, we've had a few cases recently and the only way out of it has been for the victim to pay up."

"What about the factory system? I can't stop production, Colin. We work to strict schedules. Our customers need the goods."

"That's on a different network and not at risk. My advice is to just shut the admin system down."

"We back up every evening. Can't we just reinstall as of last night?"

"No, leave everything for now. You'll need your backups if and when we free up your system. After a ransomware attack it's unlikely things will be as they were."

Eve's heart sank. She'd no idea how much this was likely to cost. She'd have to tell Simon at once. But tell him what? That she'd botched the main office system and they could no longer administer the business? The only saving grace was that the computers that controlled the labs and the factory were on a different network, and so far appeared to be unaffected.

CHAPTER 16

The moment Ruth Bayliss walked through the office door, Calladine knew something was wrong. They'd been friends and colleagues for years, and he could easily tell if something was amiss. Apart from which, her face gave her away. Her eyes were red from crying and she didn't look as if she'd slept.

"Want to talk?" he asked.

Ruth sat at her desk, shaking her head. "If you want to help, you can get me some coffee."

"Well, it's got to be bad — you look dreadful."

"It is, and I don't want to discuss it yet. I'm too shocked and upset."

Calladine made her a mug of coffee and retreated to his office, which was partitioned off from the others by frosted glass panels. Ruth had made herself clear, it was up to her if she wanted to talk. But he couldn't help checking that she was okay.

"Stop watching me," she snapped.

Not that easy, when she might need his help. They had always turned to each other whenever there was a crisis in their lives. To take his mind off Ruth, Calladine accessed Machin's record from the system. The villain had been locked away for nearly twenty years. He'd kept his nose clean, which was out of

71

character for him. And he'd taken advantage of his time inside to study for a degree in computer science. Somehow, Calladine couldn't see Clifford Machin studying for anything.

"Sorry, I don't mean to be off with you."

He looked up — Ruth was sitting at the other side of his desk sipping her coffee.

"I need to tell someone, or I'll burst. But this is for your ears only, understand?" She wagged a finger at him. "I do not want to be the subject of office gossip."

Calladine nodded.

"Jake's left me."

Blunt and hard to believe. Calladine stared at her, wondering if he'd heard her right.

"I'm not joking, Tom. A woman he works with. He's been seeing her for a while, apparently. He packed a few things last night and buggered off to hers. I got no warning. I didn't have a clue what was going on. I never suspected a thing."

Calladine had always thought that if the pair did split, it would be down to Ruth. She could be a bit flaky where the relationship was concerned.

"Are you sure it's not just a phase, some sort of crush?"

"Phase," she scoffed. "He's a grown man, Tom. Jake knows his own mind. And don't forget, we've got Harry to think of. I doubt he dived in without a second thought." He saw the look — she wanted to say more but was biting back the words.

"You mean he's not like me?"

"You said it."

"Are you up to staying?" he asked, thinking work might help. "We've got the Ramsey murder and now Moira Haigh, Gina's aunt, is missing. She was a victim of a ransomware demand and didn't pay up. It's possible she's been harmed."

"Ransomware? Who do we know that's capable of organising that little scam?"

"I have no idea. I'm having her office system looked at by our tech boys. With luck they'll come up with something."

"I know Moira Haigh has four hairdressing salons, surely whatever system she uses can't be that complex. And why target her anyway? Her hairdressing business is small fry compared with other firms I can think of. Usually they target organisations with money in the bank. Does Moira Haigh even have any money?"

Calladine shrugged. "Seeing as you're here, perhaps you'd like to find out. I imagine she uses the system for bookings, mostly. She had the work PC in her own salon, with all the appointments, accounts and stock packages on it."

"Gina might know something. Does Arron Cookson know where she's gone? The girl should be told about her aunt."

"He says not, but he's lying. It's second nature to the lad," Calladine said.

"Okay. While I look into her finances and background, what are you going to do?"

"I'm going to have another go at him. Tell him about Gina's aunt and hope he sees sense."

There was a tap on the door. It was Rocco. "I've had a look at the CCTV from the night Ramsey was killed. Cookson was telling the truth, him and Gina can be clearly seen wandering down the lane from Hopecross to Lowermill, fish and chip cartons in their hands. Sorry, boss."

"And the timescale is right?"

Rocco nodded. "I also rang that pub in Hopecross Square. They confirmed that the pair were in there all evening."

"Want to question Cookson with me? We need to know where Gina Haigh has gone, and I'm sure he knows something."

Rocco nodded. He looked at Ruth. "You okay?"

She tried to smile but there was no hiding the ravages of a sleepless night. "Fine, thanks."

"You look as if you're sickening for something."

"A bloody fight if you don't get off my back." Ruth got up and left the office.

Calladine shook his head at the young detective. "Best leave it, son — trouble at home."

CHAPTER 17

"There's no getting away from it, Arron. You've been a naughty boy," Calladine said soberly. "Dealing drugs, using kids to sell for you." He shook his head and tutted. "They're even using your flat as a distribution centre while you're locked up in here. That's serious, could get you a long sentence."

"I've told you, I'm not who you want. I'm not the main player in this. You're wasting your time threatening me, Copper."

"We're not stupid, we know you're not running the scam, Arron. That's down to Noah Ash, and we'll be speaking to him shortly. But you are a big part of what's going on."

At the sound of Ash's name, Cookson's face fell. He began to sweat. "What have you done?" he gasped. "You've dropped me right in it. I'll have a bullet in my head before I reach the end of the street."

Calladine pulled a face. "What dangerous friends you have, Arron. If I were you, I'd seriously think about making changes."

"You have to protect me!"

"We might consider it, but you'll have to give us something in return."

"What?"

"Where is Gina, and why is she hiding?"

Calladine and Rocco watched Cookson wrestle with this. "We wanted out. Gina is in hiding, so a certain person can't find her."

"You mean Ash?" Calladine asked.

"You'll get nothing until I get a promise. I won't give you any names, understand?"

"Gina's aunt is missing, and she may have been harmed. Gina might be able to help."

Cookson looked puzzled. "The people we deal with aren't interested in Moira Haigh."

"Well, someone is. D'you know anything about ransomware, Arron?"

"Not really, but that idiot that got himself killed did. He kept warning Gina about it. Told her to warn her auntie too."

"Kieron Ramsey?"

"Yeah, him. He hung out in an internet café somewhere. He told Gina he'd met a bloke who was an expert."

"Where is this internet café?" Calladine asked.

"I don't know, he never said, I wasn't that interested, to be honest."

Not much use, but it wasn't around here, because Leesdon didn't have one. "You're sure it was a café, not a library or something?"

"No, he deffo said internet café."

"This bloke Ramsey met, did he say anything about him?" Calladine asked.

"Not really, just that he was older and quiet. Didn't give much away or want to talk. But Ramsey watched him, reckoned he was up to no good."

"Gina, where is she?"

"Our plan was to hide out in a caravan on the coast near Bridlington until the drugs thing calmed down. We'd be safe there, no one round here knows about the place. She thought it was the new drugs boss who poisoned the drinks in the supermarket. Gina reckoned if we weren't around, there'd be no more trouble."

He still wasn't using names. "Ring her, tell her to expect us, and we'll bring her back," Calladine said.

Cookson nodded. "Do I get protection, then? I've told you all I can."

Calladine shook his head. "I'm still short of a name. Who is behind the drug-running, Arron? Tell me that and you will be put somewhere safe, and we'll send a uniformed officer to pick up Gina so she can join you. Once we've got whoever is behind the drug-dealing, you'll be able to resume your old life."

"I can give you a name but I've no proof. That'd be up to you to find."

"A name, Arron."

"Noah Ash."

* * *

Gina Haigh would be picked up later that day and interviewed. With luck she might have information about the internet café Ramsey had spoken to her about. Calladine returned to the office.

"Digital forensics have been on the phone, sir," Alice said.

"Who was it?"

"A Dr Roxy Atkins. She said she knew you."

Calladine was surprised. Roxy had worked with Julian at one time. What, he wondered, had prompted her to make the change to digital forensics?

He picked up the phone. "Roxy. This is a turn-up. What are you doing with the tech boys?"

"Running the show," she told him. "Didn't you wonder what had happened to me?" The line went silent for a few seconds. "You didn't . . . you didn't even notice I'd gone, did you? You don't half know how to make a girl feel needed. I re-trained, Tom, and now I'm back, and attached to the Duggan on a permanent basis."

"That's good news, Roxy. What have you got for us?"

"I looked at Moira Haigh's PC. It's locked up tight, and without the decryption key, it's well-nigh impossible to fix."

"Any clue how the PC was infected or who did it?"

"Moira had the business PC and a tablet — I presume for when she visited her other salons. She received an email purporting to be from a supplier, the virus was embedded in an attachment. She opened the email and attachment on her PC and the damage was done, but it was still unopened on the tablet. I've traced the email to a public IP address in Huddersfield."

Calladine's eyes had glazed over. What was a public IP address, for goodness' sake? "Sorry, Roxy, I never did do the IT training. I have the basics, so don't expect too much. What does that mean?"

"It means the email was sent from a public computer, a library or internet café for example. In the case of this email, it came from an internet café. I have texted you the address. It's on Meltham Road in Huddersfield."

It seemed Kieron Ramsey had got it right. Was that where he'd first met his killer? "That's great work, Roxy, thanks."

He put the phone down and looked at Ruth. "Did you get all that? Looks like you and me are taking a trip over the hills." He turned to Rocco. "Gina Haigh is holed up in a caravan in Bridlington. I'll send a couple of uniforms to pick her up. We need to know what she can tell us about Ramsey, and what he knew about a man he met in this internet café. Also, if she has any idea why her aunt was targeted."

CHAPTER 18

Calladine instructed two uniformed officers to find Noah Ash and bring him in for questioning. "He's unlikely to tell us much," he told Ruth. "All we've got is Cookson's word that Ash is behind the dealing. Still, we'll have a go at the lad and see what we get."

"Rob's been on," she said. "He's matched the paint flecks on Ramsey's clothes to Cookson's van. It had been torched but there were still enough bits of it intact to get the match. Are you sure we're not looking at Cookson for this?"

"Cookson didn't kill Ramsey. We have him on CCTV ambling along the Hopecross Road with Gina that night. I think his van was used because the lock was faulty, and everyone knew Cookson didn't mind people borrowing it whenever they chose to."

"I wonder why the killer didn't torch the van with Ramsey in it? To me that would have made more sense, and it would have messed with the forensic investigation."

Ruth had a point. "Perhaps the killer was pressed for time, about to be disturbed. It was throwing-out time for the pubs, remember, and everyone uses that spare ground as a shortcut."

He turned to Rocco. "Did you ask in the Pheasant?"

"No one heard or saw anything, sir," Rocco said. "But then no one drinking in there would admit it if they had."

"Perhaps we should give it another go," Calladine told Ruth. "Fancy some food before our jaunt over to Huddersfield? I bet you've not eaten a thing today."

"Canteen?"

Calladine nodded.

"Before you go, Ruth," Alice said. "The bank has been on the phone about Moira Haigh's finances. She has a few thousand in her account, but she still has a mortgage on the house and rents the salon properties. She's successful but not wealthy by any stretch."

"Not worth holding to ransom in that case, so why her?" Calladine thought for moment. "Would you find out if anyone along the road Moira Haigh lives on has CCTV? If so, we'd like to take a look."

"Is the ransomware incident connected to Ramsey's murder?" Ruth asked as they took the stairs.

"It's possible. According to Cookson, Ramsey spoke to Gina about a bloke in an internet café."

"That could be the motive. The killer thinks Gina knows something that implicates her boyfriend in Ramsey's killing. A warning to her to stay quiet, perhaps."

Calladine wasn't sure it was that simple. "Perhaps. We'll see what we find. We'll talk to Ash and then take a ride over to Huddersfield. I hope that internet café keeps good records." He paused for a moment. Dare he ask? She might bite his head off. "You okay, getting your head straight?"

"No, I'm not okay! My long-term partner and father to my son has just dumped me. How d'you think I feel?"

"Sorry, but I do want to help if I can."

"Well, you can't, so back off."

That told him in no uncertain terms.

There was a strong smell of onions in the staff canteen. "They've got that bloody pie on again. Mince and onion supposedly, but extra-heavy on the onion. And look at that crust, thick and full of fat. You'll have to go it alone, Tom, I can't eat the stuff in here."

"Leaving me to it, are you? Okay, run off and eat a box of salad on your own. Meet me by my car in about twenty minutes."

Calladine had no qualms about eating the canteen food. He mostly cooked for himself, so he couldn't afford to be too choosy. Food was food, and he grabbed it wherever he could. A plateful of pie and chips in hand, he scanned the room for a free chair. It was crowded, but there was one free place. The only problem was, it'd mean sitting next to Greco.

Greco smiled at Tom as he sat down. "I passed on the pie." He nodded at Calladine's heap of food. "Mind you, there's not much on the veggie counter."

"You're as bad as Ruth, she's a health freak too." Calladine could have bitten his tongue — had he really just called the new boss a *freak*? "What I mean is, she's careful about what she eats," he muttered.

"Does no harm. The weight soon creeps up."

Was that a dig at him? Calladine admitted he wasn't as trim as he should be these days, but it was hard — the job, living alone, it took its toll.

"How's the case doing? Are you any closer to finding the killer?" Greco asked.

"We're getting there. We've got people to interview and we're following several lines of enquiry."

"Ransomware. I read the report earlier. That's a tricky one and often the preserve of organised crime."

Greco had a point, but if he was right, who were they looking at? "We're taking a ride over to an internet café in Huddersfield. I'm hopeful we'll get something we can use."

"Are the cases connected? The murder of that young man and the missing woman?"

"On the surface it doesn't appear so, but we're keeping an open mind. A young woman we're bringing in was known to both." How much help Gina Haigh would be was anybody's guess, but Calladine wanted to give Greco something.

80

"Quaid was here earlier. Did he speak to you?" Greco said.

"Yes, someone I helped put away years ago has been released on licence. Quaid wanted to warn me — didn't know he cared." Calladine laughed.

Greco had that serious look on his face, the one that made him look even more of a nerd than he usually did. "Be careful, Tom. Quaid might have a point."

CHAPTER 19

The ride across Leesworth moor towards Huddersfield was the quickest route from Leesdon. It was also quite spectacular, and today, in the sunshine, it was even more enjoyable. They climbed upwards, the route bordered on one side by hills sporting grazing sheep, and on the other by a steep drop as the land tumbled away to the valley below and the huge expanse of water that was Doveclough Lake. At the top was a two-way junction. Both took you into Huddersfield but only one via Meltham.

"It's off here somewhere that Cookson's van was found," Ruth told him as they sped off along the old Meltham Road. "Odd, don't you think, leaving it so far out? I mean, ask yourself, what was the killer doing all the way up here?"

"If you want to lose a burnt-out vehicle, it's as good a place as any, I suppose."

"It doesn't seem right to me. You don't stumble on an out of the way lane like that by chance."

Ruth had a point. Calladine had grown up here and knew the area well. When he'd been a lad, he used to cycle up here and had explored extensively with his mates. "You think the killer lives locally?"

"Possibly. He doesn't appear to have any bother finding his way around the area."

"A good map would give you all the insight you needed," he said. "Let's not jump to any conclusions just yet. Sorry if I put my foot in it earlier."

"You didn't, but I'm still in shock. I never thought, not even for one minute, that Jake would leave us. I'm struggling, to be honest."

"You did argue, you said so most days," Calladine reminded her.

"I know, but a lot of that was down to me. I'm never satisfied. Jake was good at doing and saying the wrong thing and I was always on his back."

"Don't beat yourself up, Ruth. He might come back."

"I don't think so, not this time. I strongly suspect it's over, Tom. We'll both just have to get used to it." After a while, she said, "Do we know whereabouts on Meltham Road this café is? You haven't set the satnav up."

"The bloody thing does my head in, that's why. She's forever telling me to 'turn around at the next junction.' I much prefer to use my nose. We need the bit before the old road hits the town centre. We go through the lights for a few metres towards the shops and park up anywhere at the back."

"I'll keep my eyes peeled. Do we know who runs the place?"

"No, but it's bound to be some young bloke. They seem to be the only ones who know all about IT stuff these days."

"Don't be so sexist, Calladine. You're forgetting Roxy, she's an expert in that field now."

He nodded. "Sorry, forgot about her." He took a deep breath — the next bit could be tricky. Talking about Jake on the way here had made him realise that Ruth could be making one huge mistake. "Can I suggest you think carefully about your relationship with Jake? You might still put things right and that would be better for all three of you."

Ruth was very good at trying to bury things, particularly personal stuff, but she needed to face this one, and quick.

"He's left me, Tom — packed his stuff and gone. He's done all the thinking he needs to and if that's how he wants it, so be it."

"But you don't want that, not really. All this anger is because you're hurting. My advice, for what's it's worth, take time, work it through, and think about Harry."

"Harry will be fine. We'll draw up some sort of rota. Although I'll do everything I can to stop him seeing our son along with that woman."

Calladine could see trouble on the horizon. "In that case, Jake would have to see him at yours or take him out. What about when you're working well into the night and Harry needs looking after for several hours before you get home?"

"I haven't thought that far, Tom. But Harry is not going to that woman's place! Jake will just have to take care of him at ours."

Ruth was dabbing her eyes again. She was obviously finding this painful and he felt awful for bringing it up. "Sorry, I have no right to wade in. If you want to bend my ear at any time, or need my help, you know I'm here for you."

"Thanks, Tom, you're a love."

"That's it, over there." Calladine nodded. "We'll park and take a look."

* * *

Holme Internet Café was named after the Holme Valley the village was situated in. It was equipped with twenty PCs. Some were arranged on benches around the perimeter of the main room and cordoned off from each other by screens, and others sat on small desks. The premises looked clean and well maintained, but short on customers. There were only two blokes in the place. Calladine approached the counter, where a young man was struggling with the coffee machine.

"Won't be a minute. Damn thing's so temperamental it's not funny."

"It's okay, son, we're not after a drink."

"If it's a PC you want, take your pick. If it's a repair or spare part, you'll have to see the boss."

Calladine discreetly showed him his badge. "It's your boss we need a word with."

"He's out, so I'll have to do. I'm Nathan." He smiled.

Calladine retrieved the IP address that Roxy had given him from a note in his pocket. "This particular machine — do you have a record of who has used it?"

Nathan looked at a chart behind the counter and pointed to a PC on one of the desks. "It's that one there. What dates are you after?"

This was going better than Calladine had expected. Walk in, find the machine in question, and now he was about to get a name. "Can I have a list of who's used it during the past month?"

"Sure, I'll get you a printout."

"Do you delete the history?" Ruth asked.

"The customers usually do that themselves," Nathan said. "If not, then we do." He handed Calladine a sheet of paper.

Calladine's face fell. So much for it being easy. He should have known it was too good to be true. "This is rubbish, there's not a genuine name on here. Look," he pointed, "'Snowdrop.' Who's that supposed to be? And this one, 'Waldo.' What are these people afraid of?"

"That's what most people are like, I'm afraid. They don't want tracing."

"Do you have CCTV?" asked Calladine.

"No, the owner isn't a fan," Nathan said.

"Do you allow customers to use the dark net?" Ruth asked.

"No, of course not. The owner wouldn't allow anything illegal."

"But would you know if a customer did use it?"

He nodded at a large sign on the wall behind the counter. "All our customers know that we monitor usage, on a random basis. We have a master computer in the office from which we can look at any of the screens in here."

"When is he due back, this owner?" Calladine asked.

The pair heard the café door open and close. They turned, and saw an older man in an overcoat, standing with his hands in his pockets, watching them. He was of medium height and thick-set. He had sparse hair and he was clean-shaven.

"Long time no see, Calladine," he said, "but I can't say I've missed you. What are you doing on my premises?"

It was one of those rare occasions when Calladine's heart missed a beat. He knew that voice at once. He hadn't heard it in years, but it still had the power to chill his bones. The last time he'd seen him, he'd been screaming obscenities at him from the dock.

"Oh dear, the years haven't done you any favours," the man sneered. "You've piled it on and gone grey. Shame. Ray always maintained you were the looker in your family. Well, no longer, sadly."

"Machin!"

"The very same." He smiled.

My premises. The realisation hit Calladine like a blow to the guts. "You're the owner?"

Machin looked around him. "Yes, and it's doing okay too. The café, repairs and sales, we do brisk trade."

Calladine had to get his act together. He couldn't risk showing any weakness or fear in front of this man. "That's a shame, Cliff. Well, I'm sorry it's me that has to be the bearer of bad news but I'm going to have to close you down. I'm investigating a murder and the victim used this place."

CHAPTER 20

Calladine asked Ruth to drive them back. He needed time to calm himself, and he had calls to make. They hadn't left until a uniformed officer from Huddersfield had arrived to ensure the internet café remained in lockdown until Roxy Atkins took charge of the PCs.

"Who is he? You obviously know him," Ruth said.

"His name is Clifford Machin, a one-time cohort of two infamous villains, Reggie York and Ray Fallon. Machin has recently come out of prison. He is a violent thug who doesn't give a damn who he kills or hurts. Along with the other two, he used to be one of the most feared men in the North West of England. I knew he was out on licence, but I didn't expect to see him so near my own patch."

"Who told you he was out?"

"I had a visit from Quaid. He knows the history and came to warn me."

"That man wants to harm you?" Ruth asked.

"Yes, I suspect he does. He blames me for his time inside."

"What did he do?"

"Amongst other things, he killed a young man and has never said what he did with the body. He reckons it wasn't him, that it was Ray who committed the murder."

"You investigated at the time?"

"Yes, and Machin was as guilty as sin," he said.

"What's he doing slap bang in the middle of our current case then? Is he trying to implicate you in something?"

"I've no idea, but I was really shocked, Ruth, seeing him standing there after all this time. I need to think this through. Machin could be connected, he has enough contacts on the Hobfield."

"But what's his beef with Ramsey?"

"Ramsey went to that internet café. He will have no doubt met Machin. Perhaps the lad upset him in some way."

"And Moira Haigh? The email she got came from there, too. Is Machin running some sort of scam? Is that how he's making his money these days? Is it possible that Ramsey found out what he was doing, and that's why he was killed?" she asked.

Calladine fell silent. Ruth's theory was sound. If Ramsey had spotted something going on, overheard something, he would have been in danger and might have been threatened. Machin wasn't a man you crossed.

Seeing his old enemy had shaken him. If the man was involved in the case, they were in for a bumpy ride. The Machin of old, the one Calladine remembered, took no prisoners. Get in his way and you'd be disposed of.

His mobile rang. It was Roxy. "My people are looking at those PCs in the café now. I'll take the one that was used to send the emails back to the lab and glean from it what I can. The owner was none too happy, though. He blames you entirely. Reckons you've got it in for him and this is you being vindictive."

"He's wrong. That's not how I work."

"I know that, Calladine, I'm just telling you what the man said. I'll get back to you as soon as."

"Don't upset forensics," Ruth reminded him. "We need them to do their jobs so that we can do ours."

Calladine grunted. They could do with working faster, in his opinion. "We've heard precious little from that pretty face you're so into. When we get back to the station, get onto Dr Harris and tell him we need results."

Ruth sighed. "I'm sure Rob is doing his best."

"Truth is, we need Julian on the job. Someone should tell him to get his head out of the clouds and concentrate."

"Please don't start with him," she said. "You'll wade in and upset the man and then he'll go into a sulk. Remember, this is Julian we're dealing with. The forensics take time, you know that."

"If this is down to Machin, we have to have proof, and quick. The man's slippery. Believe me, Ruth, I know him of old."

Calladine leaned back and closed his eyes. Seeing Machin had dredged up all the bad memories. That kid's remains had never been found but there were photos. Images of the body in various stages of readiness for dumping. His clothing had been removed and that had never been found either — it was presumed that Machin had burnt it. Then the body had been wrapped in what looked like an old curtain and bound tight with tape. What happened to the poor lad after that was anybody's guess. Machin swore the photos had been sent to him anonymously, but Calladine had never believed that. They were trophies, pure and simple. But nothing could be proved either way. There was nothing to be gleaned from those pictures that could point to location either, and Machin had simply shrugged them off as an example of Fallon's bad taste.

"He did a computing degree inside, Quaid told me," Calladine said. "So, he has the expertise but what's his motive? Perhaps you're right, ransomware is how Machin intends to expand his bank account. The internet café might be a good little business but it won't make big money."

"Perhaps that's not what he wants. He's done his time. He most likely wants to be left alone to get on with his life," Ruth said.

"You don't know him like I do. Him and Fallon, plus York, were very bad. Three killers without a conscience. I'm sure Machin hasn't changed that much. He's just better at hiding it."

CHAPTER 21

"We found Noah Ash in the pub in Hopecross Square. He put up quite a fight — jumped into his car and made off down the Lowermill Road," Rocco was saying. Calladine was back at the station.

"But you caught him?"

"He crashed into the bollards at the end of Mill Brow. Idiot must have forgotten there's no access that way."

"Was he hurt?"

"Only his pride, and that car of his has a few dents. He's got some temper on him, I'll say that. Lunged at me and Constable Heap. The constable did a breath test, which Ash failed. He's currently cooling off in the cells while we wait for the blood test results."

"Good work, catching him. We'll talk to him shortly."

Calladine wanted a coffee and a break to take stock. He was still reeling from his encounter with Machin.

But before he had a chance to retreat to his office, Alice told him Eve Buckley wanted him to ring her. "She said it's urgent."

Urgent or not, Calladine couldn't face making small talk with Eve just now. He needed to be alone to think.

"Do you want me to interview Ash with you?" Ruth asked.

"No, it'll be me and Rocco," Calladine said. "Why don't you get off early? Speak to Jake, try and sort things out."

Ruth pulled a face. "I think we're way past that, Tom, but I'd appreciate the early dart. Are you okay?"

"No, but I'll get over it. I just have to get used to the idea that Machin is so close by and free to operate as he pleases."

"See you tomorrow then."

Calladine went into his office, closed the door behind him and sat sipping his coffee. What to do about Machin? The man knew about computers, networks and systems, which was key to their current case. Ramsey had used Machin's internet café, and Moira Haigh, the aunt of one of Ramsey's friends, had been targeted with ransomware. In Calladine's book, that meant that the villain had to be involved in their case. But was he the killer? And if so, what was his motive?

His phone rang. It was Quaid.

"You've seen Machin, I hear. Not a wise move, Tom. The man has made a complaint, reckons you're harassing him."

"He's wrong. The internet café he runs is part of our current investigation. We went along to have a chat and ask about customers who use it. I had no idea that Clifford Machin had anything to do with the place."

"Is he a suspect?"

As far as Calladine was concerned, yes, he was currently their prime suspect, but Quaid didn't need to know that yet. "We're waiting for IT forensics, sir, and then we'll know more."

"Okay, keep me up to date with progress, Tom. In the meantime, let the man reopen, that'll keep him off my back. And if it looks likely that Machin is to be questioned, get Greco to sit in. We do not want him filing an official complaint against you."

Calladine felt as if he'd just had his hands tied. Bloody Machin! There was a knock on his door.

"Ash is kicking off, sir," said Rocco. "His solicitor has turned up and is demanding to see you."

"Okay, me and you will speak to him."

Calladine checked his reflection in the mirror on his office wall. Machin was right, he had gone to seed. Losing weight would help, and he needed to get a lot fitter.

The two detectives walked along the corridor towards the interview room. "Who's he got with him?" Calladine asked.

"Justin Falkner. He's from that large practice in Oldston."

Calladine knew who he was. He represented Eve and he'd met him on a couple of occasions.

Falkner greeted him. "Tom. Hope you're well, it's been a while." He smiled. "Can we get this business sorted quickly? My client is only too happy to help with anything he can."

Smarmy git! Happy to help indeed. Falkner had no idea.

"Tell me about the drug dealing on the Hobfield," Calladine began.

"No comment," Ash said with a grin.

"We have information that you are running the show, Noah."

"No bloody comment!"

Falkner butted in. "There's no need to be rude, Noah. And I'd advise you to answer DI Calladine's questions as fully as you can."

The look Noah Ash gave his brief was poisonous. "He's only here because my mother hired him. Afraid he's got a lot to learn." He grinned again.

"Forensics are searching your car," Calladine told him. "Will they find anything?"

The young man shrugged. "If they do, I didn't put it there. Perhaps I'm being set up. Nice guy like me — good home, money." He smiled. "People get jealous and they put the boot in."

"Arron Cookson — he works for you. What about Kieron Ramsey? Did you know him?"

That woke Ash up. The grin vanished. Now he looked worried. "That guy who was killed? I wasn't involved. Try pinning that on me and you'll come off worst."

"Is that a threat, Noah?"

Before he got chance to reply, there was a knock at the door. It was Alice. Calladine went out into the corridor to see what she wanted.

"Forensics have gone over Noah Ash's car thoroughly and found nothing drug-related," she said.

"They gave the boot a thorough going-over?"

"Yes, nothing but some shopping. The receipt in the carrier bag was dated yesterday. All looks fine, nothing suspicious."

That was a shame. Calladine had been hoping for a break.

CHAPTER 22

Day 4

Eve Buckley had a sleepless night. She had recovered from the initial horror of being targeted with ransomware, but she and Simon still couldn't administer the business. Within an hour of the attack, the screens were flashing instructions on payment and a deadline. She and Simon agreed that they wouldn't pay. Instead they handed the problem over to Colin and the company he worked for. After an initial examination, he'd seemed hopeful. The question now was whether to report it to the police. Perhaps a word with Tom, see what he advised.

The problem was getting hold of him. She'd left numerous messages for Tom to ring her, but so far, he hadn't. Eve decided that if he hadn't contacted her by midday, she'd visit him at the station. Meanwhile, there was nothing to be done in the office, so she decided to visit Zoe in Lowermill. She was about to leave when she heard a man call out to her from the front gates.

"Excuse me! There's a distressed cat out here."

Eve groaned. It would be Bubbles from next door. The animal was always wandering off, oblivious to the perils of traffic. Eve hoped she hadn't been hit by something.

Eve walked down her drive. She'd have a look, see if she could raise her neighbour. "Is she injured?" she asked.

"Doesn't look good. It's lying in the gutter and hasn't moved."

"Used up all her nine lives then." Eve grimaced. She went out into the lane. She bent over, looking around for the animal but could see nothing. "Could she have sneaked off?"

He didn't answer.

Eve didn't see the blow coming. Still looking at the ground, she felt something strike her head. Then, nothing.

* * *

"Come on, Noah, where do you keep the stuff?" Calladine demanded.

"Get off my back. I'm not involved. I keep telling you, but you don't listen. Get it into your thick skull, the dealing has nothing to do with me!" Noah Ash protested.

"We know that's not true. A witness has named you and one of my own team can vouch for your car being on the Hobfield last night while dealing was taking place." The young man was silent. He looked pensive. "Lie to us now and we find something later on, it won't go well for you. I can easily get a warrant to search your home."

"I'm not lying," Ash said. "And leave my parents out of this. I don't want them worrying."

"You could simply tell me who supplies you and save us all a lot of bother."

The lad was silent again. He seemed to be weighing this up. Ash looked drained, a night in the cells hadn't suited him at all. Calladine had hoped that it would make him a bit more forthcoming today.

"I work for myself and I don't take orders from no one."

"I know you're supplying most of Leesworth, Noah. Tell me who is helping you."

"Even if I was guilty, there's no way I'd tell you that."

"Suit yourself. That means you'll stay with us a little longer. We have further enquiries to make."

Ash looked at his solicitor. "You're supposed to help me, aren't you? Do something!"

"It's as DI Calladine says, Noah. They have a witness who has named you."

"He's lying! They can't take the word of some scrote and not believe what I say!"

"My advice is to help the inspector, tell him what you know. If they are satisfied, you will get bail. If not—"

Noah Ash suddenly went pale and clutched at his chest. "I need my inhaler."

From the noise he was making, this wasn't put on. Just what they needed — the lad was asthmatic. "Did you have it with you when you were brought in?" asked Calladine.

Ash nodded, and Calladine instructed one of the uniforms to go and find it.

"Take it easy, Noah, breathe slowly," Falkner said. He turned to Calladine. "My client should see a doctor."

Ash was gasping for every breath, so Calladine didn't have much choice. "I'll get someone to take a look at you."

The uniformed constable returned with Ash's inhaler and the lad grabbed it. "I haven't had an attack like this in ages," he rasped. "It's all your bloody fault, putting me under pressure like this."

"Calm down," Falkner advised. "Getting angry doesn't help, Noah. Take a sip of water."

"How d'you feel now?" Calladine asked.

"Half dead. It always takes it out of me. I'm scared stiff I won't be able to breathe at all."

"Can I suggest you bail my client and I'll take him to A & E. I will ensure he returns if need be," Falkner said.

Calladine watched Ash carefully. It was obvious that he was genuinely ill. His mouth was open and he was gasping for every breath. He had little choice but to ensure the lad got medical attention fast. "Abscond and I'll have you locked up with no chance of getting out. Got that, Noah?"

The lad nodded. He seemed to be unable to speak. He was still a ghastly white.

"I'll take him to A & E myself," Falkner said.

"Keep in touch," Calladine said. "Let me know what the doctor says about his condition."

So much for that. Calladine was certain the dealing was down to Ash but he couldn't risk him getting dangerously ill while trying to prove it. He returned to the main office.

"Simon Buckley has been on the phone. He wants you to ring him urgently," Alice said.

Simon? Calladine and his half-brother weren't particularly close. What did he want?

Calladine retreated to his office and rang him back.

"Have you seen my mother?" Simon asked straight away.

Calladine was tempted to remind him that she was his mother too but resisted. Simon sounded very worried. "No. Why?"

"She's missing. Her car is on the drive, door swinging in the breeze, and the front gate's open, but there's no sign of her. It looks to me as if she was about to leave but somehow got distracted or called away. I've tried her mobile, but no answer."

"She's not next door? Or walking the dog?"

"She'd never leave the car open like that, as well as the gate and the front door. Anyone could have walked in. I'm worried, Tom. I think something has happened to her. I don't know if she told you, but our firm is currently the target of ransomware."

CHAPTER 23

"Trouble?" Ruth asked when Calladine reappeared.

"I'm not sure, but Simon seems to think so."

"Go on, what's happened?"

"Eve seems to have disappeared. It may or may not be related but Buckley Pharmaceuticals is currently the victim of a ransomware demand."

Ruth was shocked. "You'll have to tell Greco. Eve's your mother and if anything has happened to her, he won't allow you to be involved in this."

He shook his head. He'd tell Greco when he was good and ready. He had one or two ideas of his own. One of them was to involve Roxy, get her to look at Buckley's admin system.

"You can't leave this, Tom, Eve could be in danger. You have no choice but involve Greco and leave him to get Roxy on the job."

"And I will, but nothing is certain yet. There has been a demand to free the system, but nothing about Eve being in any danger. She may be perfectly alright."

"Have it your own way but I think you're making a mistake. This will have come as a shock, a bit like Jake splitting with me."

"I'll sort it, but I need to get my head straight first," he replied.

"Gina Haigh is in the soft interview room with Arron Cookson. Are you up to having a word now, or what?"

"We need to gather as much evidence as possible against Noah Ash, and we need their cooperation, so we go easy. We have nothing on Gina, and Cookson is out on bail."

"Falkner's been on the phone. Ash has been admitted. Not been taking his meds, apparently. Preferred smoking weed instead."

"Silly boy. At least we know where he is. Ramsey had asthma too. I wonder if the pair ever met."

"You think Ash killed Ramsey?"

"No. The attack on Ramsey was deliberately drawn out and calculated. But we'll keep the connection in mind." He checked his mobile. It was just possible that Eve had tried to contact him. Yesterday she had, he remembered, and now he regretted not getting back to her. "Come on then, let's see what this pair have to say for themselves."

"You look worried. Eve will turn up. There will be a simple explanation," Ruth said.

Arron and Gina were with a uniformed constable, drinking coffee.

Calladine smiled at them. "Hello, Arron. This is Gina, I take it."

Gina Haigh wasn't someone you'd pass in the street and not notice. She had vivid green-and-black hair with matching heavily made-up eyes. Calladine sat down opposite them and waded straight in. "Do you know where your aunt is, Gina?"

The girl looked at him as if he was stupid. "My auntie has a mind of her own. Doesn't tell me anything and goes where she likes. She could be anywhere."

"We're concerned that she might have been harmed. Her computer — the one she uses for her business — was attacked by ransomware."

Gina's face broke into a wide smile. "Serves the bitch right. Has she paid up?"

"No, I don't think she has, which is why we're worried. Has she tried to contact you during the past couple of days?"

"No, and I wouldn't worry. The disappearing act will be her way of wriggling out of it. Someone wants money and that's what Moira does — scarpers."

Calladine wasn't getting anywhere on the subject of the girl's aunt. "Tell me about Noah Ash," he asked them.

"He's a prat," said Gina at once.

Calladine nodded at Cookson. "I got the impression that your boyfriend is afraid of him. What do you say, Arron?"

Arron Cookson looked at Gina. "Look, G, I told the inspector what I know. Noah deals drugs and works with some dodgy people."

"Which is why we should keep our gobs shut," she said, nudging him. "You grass on Noah and we're dead — you know how it works. There've been enough warnings."

"Warnings? What warnings?" Ruth asked.

"I think he was behind the poisoning in the supermarket. It was Noah's way of letting me and Cooksie know he was in charge and could cause trouble."

"So why protect him? Tell us what you know, and he won't be able to bother you again," Ruth said.

Gina looked doubtful. "It's not just Noah, though, is it?"

"Tell us about the chain of supply, Gina," Calladine said. "We know Ash supplies the likes of Arron and others, but the man I want is whoever supplies Ash. Do you have any idea who that is?"

"No. Noah would never say. I did ask him, but he clammed up, said we were better off not knowing because he was one real tough nut. But the bloke did ring him once when me and Cooksie were with him."

"On his own mobile?" Ruth asked.

"He's not that stupid. It'll have been a burner."

"How long ago?" asked Ruth.

"Last week some time."

Calladine looked at Ruth. It could be that that phone was still in use and hidden, ready for the next time.

"You must have rung Noah, Arron," Calladine said. "Want to give me the number?"

"No. Can't remember it."

"No matter, we have your records."

Calladine reminded himself to ask about them when they returned to the main office.

"Is there owt else?" Gina asked.

"Not for now. Thanks, both of you."

"What are you going to do with us now? He might deserve locking up — he's admitted stuff — but not me. I've done nowt," Gina said.

"I want you both to think carefully about the things you haven't told us. I want information about the dealing — names and dates. Tell me what you know and we'll keep you safe until this is over," Calladine said. "Meanwhile, you're free to go, Gina. Arron, I'd remind you that you're still on bail. Make a run for it and we'll haul you back in and until your case comes up in court, you'll spend the rest of the waiting time in the cells."

"You have to protect us now," Cookson protested. "We step outside and they could be waiting. No, I've told you everything I know. You have to put us somewhere safe. Now."

"Okay, we'll find a place for you both."

CHAPTER 24

Back in the main office, Calladine took a call from Roxy Atkins. Her tone was upbeat and her cheerful voice lifted his mood. "You've got something?" he asked.

"Yes, I've been going through the hard drive of that PC we brought in from the internet café," Roxy replied.

"Go on, surprise me. Was it Dopey or Waldo who sent that email?"

"Neither. It was an individual using the name 'Snowdrop.' We checked the café's records and the good bit is he used that keyboard last. Which means that with care, we should get partial prints and DNA."

"Roxy, you're a star, you've brightened my day. Have you passed the keyboard on to Julian?"

"No, I've given the job to Rob. But don't worry, Tom, he knows what he's doing."

"Anything else?"

"Snowdrop did use the dark web and that's where he got the encryption codes from. He appears to have done a deal with a group in Romania."

"Any chance of getting the codes to solve the problem?"

"I doubt it," she said. "The code will have cost and been paid for in bitcoin. But if I do get anything else, you'll be the first to know."

Calladine wrote the name on the incident board and underlined it. "This is the joker who nobbled Moira Haigh's system. Anyone knows this nickname or hears it used on the street, we need to know," he told the team.

He saw Ruth yawn. Her mind wasn't on the case. Given her personal problems, he understood why. "Get off home," he told her. "And try to have that conversation with Jake. If nothing else, the pair of you need to sort who sees Harry and when."

He saw the look. She was less than impressed with that idea.

"You don't look so clever yourself. Found Eve yet?"

Calladine realised he'd no idea if she'd turned up or not. "I'll ring Simon shortly and find out."

"Get a grip, Calladine, she's your mother. Anything could have happened to her."

"No, this is Eve we're on about. It's more likely she's gone shopping with a friend."

"Sir." A uniformed officer called from the doorway. "There's a woman asking for you downstairs."

"Does she have a name?"

"Emma Holden."

Ruth gave him a smirk. "Go on then. Take her for a drink, see what she wants."

"Might I remind you, Sergeant Bayliss, that Miss Holden knew Kieron Ramsey and she might have information we can use."

"Excuses," Ruth scoffed. "You fancy her because she reminds you of Lydia. Admit it, Calladine."

"You really think I'm that shallow? You think I could only like this woman because of her resemblance to her sister?"

"Yes, I do. I know you of old, remember. Word of warning. Take her for a drink, talk about Lydia but don't get yourself in too deep. You'll only regret it."

* * *

Calladine had to admit that Emma Holden's likeness to her sister was uncanny, not just in her features but in the way she dressed.

She greeted him with a smile. "I owe you an apology. I wasn't very nice the other day, and it's been preying on my mind."

"It's okay." Calladine shrugged it off. "I'm not one for holding grudges."

"Do you want to go for a drink?" she asked.

The invitation was exactly what he needed. "The Wheatsheaf across the road is okay, and it does good food too."

"Okay, I'm up for that. I think we need to have a chat about Lydia, don't you? We should clear the air."

Did that mean Emma didn't blame him for her sister's death after all? Possibly not. After all, he still blamed himself for not keeping hold of her.

"Lydia was ambitious and single-minded," Emma said abruptly.

"I had noticed."

"She was fixated on that cousin of yours, and wouldn't be dissuaded from chasing a story about him."

"I did try to warn her that Ray Fallon was dangerous, but Lydia didn't want to hear."

She turned to him. "He had her killed. Shot dead in broad daylight. What sort of man does that?"

"A villain with no conscience."

"Or one who wanted to teach *you* a lesson," she said pointedly. "He knew you loved her. Killing Lydia was the perfect way of getting back at you."

So there it was. Emma Holden did blame him for Lydia's death.

CHAPTER 25

As soon as they were inside the Wheatsheaf, Calladine ordered a whisky and downed it one. If this was going to be a scathing attack, he needed his mind numb. Their meals arrived, for Calladine his favourite steak and chips, but he just pushed it around the plate. Emma, on the other hand, was tucking into her salad.

"Did you bring Lydia here?" she asked.

"Frequently. She was good company," Calladine said.

"Unlike me, you mean." She smiled. "I'm sorry if you're not enjoying this, but it's difficult for me too. Lydia and me were close. Her death hit all of her family hard."

"You do know that there was nothing I could have done, don't you? Lydia was a free spirit. I didn't want her to leave, but by then she'd had it with me and took off."

"I'm not laying the blame at your feet, Tom. You will have been as cut up at her death as the rest of us, I'm sure. I come to Leesdon occasionally and I had already decided to seek you out. I reckoned we had unfinished business and needed to talk."

"I'd no idea Lydia even had a sister," he said.

"Frightened of you wanting to meet us and being put off, I expect." Emma laughed and shook her head.

"You told me before that you came to Leesdon because of Kieron Ramsey. Did you know him well?" Calladine asked.

"Reasonably well, on a professional basis. I think he saw me as a friendly ear. He was a dreamer, was Kieron, his head was full of all sorts. I'm not sure working in a supermarket really suited him. Computers were more his thing. He lived on the internet and he was good, too. He could find anything, trace anyone."

"I know he visited an internet café in Huddersfield. I'm surprised he didn't have a laptop of his own," Calladine said.

"He told me he couldn't afford one, or broadband."

"Did he ever talk about the internet café, or the people he met there?"

She nodded. "He said he liked the company. He became friendly with some bloke who was teaching him how to code."

"Does this bloke have a name?"

"They were a weird lot, didn't use their own names. Something to do with the owner wanting him and the customers to remain anonymous. Kieron called himself Waldo and his friend was Snowdrop."

Calladine froze. A further and more positive link between Kieron's murder, the ransomware and Moira Haigh's disappearance. "Did he know this 'Snowdrop' well?"

"I don't think so," she said. "He was just pleased to be making friends with people who shared a similar interest."

"Did he say anything else about the man, like his age, what he looked like? The smallest detail might help us."

Emma gave him a quizzical look. "What is this? Why is Snowdrop so important?"

"He's involved in the case we're investigating, including Kieron's murder. I think Kieron saw or heard something at the internet café and that's what got him killed."

"Lydia always said you had a vivid imagination." She laughed. "'Never a dull moment with Tom,' she'd tell me over the phone. Kieron was a lonely young man who got unlucky one night. He was obsessed with computers but I'm sure he would steer clear of trouble."

Calladine heard his mobile buzz in his jacket pocket. "Excuse me, I'll have to get this." It was Simon Buckley, his half-brother.

"I told you earlier that Buckley Pharmaceuticals has been hit by ransomware," Simon began without preamble. "Our office systems are currently useless. Our IT people are trying to fix the problem, but they are not hopeful. We've been asked to pay the equivalent of one million pounds in bitcoin, Tom. An extortionate amount that we can't raise, and the deadline has passed. Mum still hasn't turned up, the demand and her disappearance have to be connected."

Calladine pushed his plate to the other side of the table. He felt sick. There was no way he could eat anything now. If this followed the same pattern as with Moira Haigh, Eve was in deep trouble. Moira had disappeared off the face of the earth. He needed a word with Greco.

"When did you see her last?" he asked.

"This morning, when I left for work. I had an appointment with Colin from the IT company we use. I rang her about eleven to give her an update but got no response. I've asked Samantha, and your Zoe, but no one has seen her."

"What about the neighbours?"

"Nothing, but because of the distance between the houses, they can't see onto our drive or us theirs. You can't see the lane at the bottom from the windows either."

"I'll alert uniform. They'll keep an eye out for her," Calladine said without much hope.

"I'm worried, Tom. Samantha's frantic. She reckons something dreadful has happened, that it's payback for not paying the ransom."

Calladine knew there was every chance she was right. He'd had a bad feeling about Moira Haigh from the beginning. "Assure her that we will do our very best. We'll find her."

Giving Emma an apologetic smile, he tapped in Greco's number and told him about Eve.

"We need to talk, Tom. I'll wait for you in my office."

CHAPTER 26

The last thing Ruth wanted was a row with Jake, but they did have things to discuss. She rang him on the way to the car park. "Want to go somewhere? Talk things through?"

"Sorry, Ruth. I know it's important, but Orla wants me to meet her parents. Her mum's cooking a meal and it's a chance for me to get to know them."

"I don't want to talk about us, if that's what you're worried about. I've no intention of asking you to come back. It's Harry we should think about. Stop being so selfish and think about your son for once! If Orla has anything about her, she'll understand."

"I can't talk to you when you're in this mood, Ruth. Perhaps tomorrow. I'll speak to Orla, see what she says."

So that was how it was going to be. Jake wouldn't make a move without Orla Gray's say-so. Well, stuff him! She'd make arrangements for Harry herself and if that didn't include Jake, so be it. If he was no longer part of the child's life, he only had himself to blame. She put her mobile away.

"Ruth!" A man called to her. It was Rob Harris. "I've just been up to the office to drop the latest report off for Calladine."

"I'm just off. Had enough for one day," she said. "I love my job, but it does get you down at times."

He smiled. "You need a night out, cheer you up."

She shook her head. "You make it sound so simple, but you've no idea."

"Then tell me. Let me buy you supper and we'll talk. You can sound off about your problems and I'll tell you mine."

Ruth brightened up. It was a lovely idea, but what about childcare? Then again, she was curious. What problems could Rob possibly have? From her point of view, the scientists at the Duggan were the dream team. "You already have problems? Working with Julian not suiting you? He is a bit of an acquired taste, I'm afraid."

He nodded. "I'll get used to him in time. You seem to have managed."

"Oh, we love Julian. We think of him as one of *our* team." She laughed. "He's even fathered Calladine's grandchild."

He smiled at this. "I think there must be a tale there. Have supper with me, and we can talk."

"You have my mobile number. Ring me in an hour and if I can make arrangements for my son, it's a deal." Smiling, Ruth watched him walk off towards his car. What was the harm? She deserved a bit of fun after the trauma Jake had caused her. Perhaps things weren't so grim after all.

* * *

It took her only ten minutes to drive home. Anna from across the road, Harry's regular babysitter when she and Jake were working, had picked Harry up from nursery and was waiting for her in the kitchen. She'd given the little boy his tea and the two of them were playing with his cars.

"You're wonderful with him, Anna, and I'm so grateful for your help. But I can't keep putting on you like this. With Jake no longer living here, I'll have to sort out a permanent arrangement for Harry."

"Why not make me part of that arrangement?" Anna said. "I've taken early retirement and I'm bored at home all day with nothing to do. Seeing to Harry is a joy. I love taking him to and from nursery and speaking to all the other mothers."

"You would be perfect, Anna, but my job keeps me out until all hours at times."

"I only live across the road, Ruth."

"I'd pay you the going rate, whatever that is. And then there's Jake. He'll want to see his son regularly — I hope."

"We can deal with all that," Anna said.

Ruth saw from the eagerness in Anna's face that she wanted this. Her own son was grown up and had moved to Devon, so she saw little of him. "Okay, you're on. I'll make a list of my shifts, but I have to warn you they do change."

"Not a problem. Are you working tonight?" Anna asked.

Ruth smiled. "No, but I have a date. I'll be out a couple of hours, tops. What d'you say? Are you able to stay?"

"It'll do you good. Go and get yourself ready. I'll bath Harry shortly and pop him into bed."

Half an hour later, having showered and done her hair and make-up, Ruth was waiting in her drive for Rob to pick her up. She had butterflies in her tummy. For goodness' sake! She was a grown woman.

* * *

Rob took her to the new Italian restaurant in Hopecross — very upmarket, and a far cry from the Wheatsheaf.

"You look lovely," Rob said.

She had no idea how to respond. In the end, a shy smile was all she could muster. Ruth felt nervous. It was a long time since she'd been out with a new man. She'd agonised over what to wear but had settled for a dress she'd bought last month for a friend's birthday party. It fitted her slender figure perfectly, and matching heels completed the look.

Rob poured them both a glass of red wine. "Do you like your job?"

"Love it. I can't imagine doing anything else. You?"

"I'm still making up my mind. I'm not sure the hands-on involvement with detective work suits me. All that desperation for results." He winked at her.

"It's those results that win cases in court," she said. "We've been lucky. Julian is a stickler for perfection, and over the years that has made our jobs so much easier."

"And now you've got me. I do hope I live up to expectations."

"Julian interviewed you, so he must have been impressed. He doesn't suffer fools and respects hard work. Do you think you'll stay at the Duggan?"

For a few moments, he had a wistful look in his eyes. Ruth reached out and took his hand. "Something's not right, is it? Want to share? I'm not a gossip. I can keep stuff to myself."

"There's no fooling you, is there?" He grinned. "But then you are a detective. You're right. I like the job more than I thought I would. The problem is, I'm not ready to put down roots yet. It's not my style to stay long in any one place. For months, I've had my eye on what for me would be the perfect job with a company in Switzerland, and it's always been my plan to jump ship whenever a suitable post comes up."

Ruth's heart sank. "And here we are just getting to know each other."

"I haven't gone yet, and who knows, I might change my mind and stay. I have a feeling that the Duggan and the people I'm getting to know will grow on me. And that is saying something. I'm not a people person, as a rule. Trust issues from my childhood."

Ruth was curious. "Want to talk about it?"

"Let's just say I had a traumatic time of it growing up. I hated school and was constantly being moved because of bullying."

"I'm sorry, Rob. Wasn't there anyone to help you?"

"Eventually, yes. An older and much tougher friend put a stop to the rough stuff and the name calling. He taught me how to fight back, but the experience left its mark. I tend not to stay long anywhere, and relationships scare me."

"What about your parents, couldn't they help you?"

"There was only my mother and she had no sympathy at all. When I explained what was happening to me, she said I should grow up and sort out the bullies myself. She was too taken up with running her business and making money to be bothered with me."

"I'm sorry, that's very sad, but there must have been someone in your life," she said. "A good-looking bloke like you can't fail to have female admirers."

"Kind of you to say so, but you're wrong. I'm not usually interested in starting relationships, and I think women pick up on that. But when I met you, I felt different." He paused, looking at her. "We have something, Ruth, and I know you feel it too."

Ruth didn't know what to say. She'd just come out of one relationship and although she did find Rob attractive, this was moving a bit too fast for her. She saw this as a date, an evening with a colleague, nothing else, not yet anyway. "Let's take it slowly," she said, "see where we are in a few weeks." His face fell. "I'm not sure if you're aware, but my long-term partner has just left me for someone else. I'm still in shock, to be honest, hence my hesitation to dive into a new relationship. And I have a son. He's only a toddler and has to come first."

Rob nodded, sipping his wine. What was he thinking? Ruth had no idea what was going on in that head of his. She decided to give personal matters a rest for now. "Are you enjoying the job?"

"So far, it's been fine. Dr Atkins is a little brusque. She wants things at once and isn't shy of saying so."

That surprised Ruth. Calladine and she had always found Roxy great to work with, very keen, and she understood exactly what was needed. Their current case was a prime example.

"Julian and Roxy both have their individual styles of working, but they're excellent forensic scientists. If I was in your position, Rob, I'd consider myself lucky to have them as colleagues."

CHAPTER 27

Day 5

First thing Friday morning, Calladine called a briefing in the incident room. "Eve Buckley is missing," he began. "Her company has been targeted by ransomware and the hackers are asking an extortionate sum to release it. The deadline has passed, and I believe Eve's disappearance is suspicious. It has followed the same pattern as that of Moira Haigh, who didn't pay up either."

"You must hand this aspect of the case over, Tom." Greco said from the back of the room. "Can I suggest that I investigate what has happened to your mother?"

Calladine knew he didn't have much choice. After their conversation last night there was no way Greco would sanction him continuing an investigation into a relative. "Rocco, you help DCI Greco," he said. "I have already alerted uniform, and they will report back to this team with anything they find. In the meantime, Ruth and I will have another word with Clifford Machin. We've been given some new information which may help with Kieron Ramsey's murder."

He said nothing about it also being linked to the ransomware. Greco was a good detective, but Eve was his mother, and he wasn't going to be sidelined. He would continue the investigation in his own way.

"Would you tell the family to expect us at their offices later today, Tom?" Greco said.

"Eve only works on a Wednesday. I think the blackmailer must have known that, given the attack happened on her watch. Eve is the major shareholder and would have the final say-so about parting with the money. She will have blamed herself for opening that email. The guilt will have played on her mind. The PC from the internet café has gone to IT forensics and the keyboard's been passed onto Julian's team. We're hopeful they'll give us something."

Greco nodded. "We'll visit the Buckley offices and speak to whoever was with Mrs Buckley when the attack happened," he said to Rocco.

Ruth saw from Calladine's face that he was keeping something back. Once Greco was out of the way, she tackled him. "Come on, what are you not saying?"

"I had a drink with Emma Holden last night and she told me something about Kieron. He had a friend at that internet café, went by the nickname of 'Snowdrop.'"

Ruth nodded. "You've written it on the board. How does it fit in?"

"Roxy said the email sent to Moira Haigh had come from some chancer calling himself Snowdrop, so you can join up the dots."

"So that's why we're going back. You're going to tackle Machin about this?" she asked.

"Too bloody right I am. He knows the oddballs who use his place. Kieron Ramsey and Snowdrop spent a lot of time there. And I know from Roxy's investigation of that computer that Machin's customers did use the dark web. He lied to us. Let's see how he wriggles out of that one."

"First off, we need to know who this Snowdrop really is," she said. "We get a description, show him some photos, but who do you suggest?"

"Noah Ash for a start, and Arron Cookson. After that, we'll go from there. If we get no joy, then I want a comprehensive description from Machin."

Alice interrupted them. "Sir, Professor Batho wants to speak to you."

"We'll leave as soon as I've sorted Julian," Calladine told Ruth. "Alice, has the call log from Cookson's mobile come through yet?"

"I'll check," she said. "If not, I'll wake them up a bit."

Calladine went into his office to ring Julian. He hoped it wasn't about the baby. He needed Julian's complete focus on the case right now.

Fortunately, Julian appeared to be back in work mode. "I've had a look at the keyboard Roxy passed to Rob," he said. "Rob is off today so I collected it from his lab. Unfortunately, it's yielded very little, certainly no prints and nothing I can use to get a DNA result from."

"Keyboards are usually covered in all sorts of gunk," Calladine said. "What are you saying? That someone wiped it?"

"Yes. It was probably done in that café. The machines are most likely cleaned down each night."

Was that Machin covering his tracks? "Give it another going-over, Julian. Currently it's all we've got, and things are desperate. Eve is missing, and saying I'm worried doesn't cover it."

"I will do my best, Tom."

Calladine finished the call and turned to Ruth. "Julian seems to be back on form. He reckons the keyboard isn't much use forensics-wise."

"I thought Rob was looking at that," Ruth said.

"He's not in."

"Oh. We had dinner last night. He didn't say anything about taking the day off."

Calladine gave her an odd look. "You went out with the man?" He shook his head. "I suppose it was only a matter of time. Like him, do you? How long before he takes Jake's spot in your life?"

Ruth whacked him one. "Get off my case, Calladine. You've got no room to talk. What about you and the lovely Miss Holden, eh? You seem to forget you've got Amy at home."

"That was work. You and pretty boy are something else. It won't last, you know. And Amy is a friend who's staying with me, nothing else."

"So you say," she said huffily. "And me and Rob might last. We got on fine and we'll do it again. Don't stick your nose into my business, Calladine, I'm not in the mood."

"Bugger off, Bayliss."

CHAPTER 28

"How can this place make any money? We've been here twice now, and both times it's been almost empty," Calladine said.

"I don't know, Tom. But one way or another it must pay the overheads, and Nathan's wage," said Ruth.

Calladine was suspicious. Machin was a tricky character. He might give the appearance of sticking to the rules of his licence but if anyone could find a way round them, it was him.

"Back again. People will talk." Machin, dressed in overalls, appeared from the side room and proceeded to mop the floor. "Watch you don't slip. I'm not sure my insurance is up to it."

"I'd like another word, Cliff. Won't keep you long," said Calladine.

"This is getting boring. I've only been out a matter of months and you're on my tail already."

"I want you to tell me about the clientele you get here. The one who calls himself Snowdrop, for example."

"He's just some bloke, I suppose. Can't bring him to mind. I take their money, I don't take a description." Machin shook his head and carried on mopping.

Calladine had had enough. He snatched the mop from Machin's hands and leaned on it. "Snowdrop, Cliff. Describe him. And stop pissing me about. You're on licence, you know what that means."

Machin gave Calladine a filthy look. "That you can have me back inside with a snap of your fingers." He moved closer to the detective and stared into his eyes. "But don't even think about it."

"Is that a threat, Cliff?"

"A suggestion, that's all. What d'you want to know?" Machin said.

"Who is this Snowdrop?"

"Haven't got a clue. He's only been here a couple of times, tops. Used that PC over there, the one your forensics people butchered." He nodded at a desk. "He paid the fee, probably drank a couple of coffees and then buggered off."

Calladine handed Machin the photos. "Have a look at these. Do you recognise either of them as Snowdrop?"

"No, but then I wouldn't, would I? I don't remember the man."

"I hope you're not messing me around, Cliff. Obstructing an investigation is an offence."

Calladine showed him a photo of Ramsey.

"Yeah, he used to come here. Quiet lad. Him and another lad got into a bust-up one day, haven't seen him since."

"D'you know who he argued with?" Calladine asked.

"No, just another customer."

"This Snowdrop. Are you sure you don't have a proper name for him?"

"I told you, that's not how we run this place."

"Fair enough, but why do your clients use nicknames?" Ruth asked. "Is it because they're up to no good?"

"They pay the fee, sit down and get on with it. I don't ask questions. I don't know what folk use places like this for, but they do. What I do know is they like anonymity and that's fine by me."

"What about payment?" Ruth asked. "Surely some of them must have paid by card?"

Calladine smiled. Clever Ruth, why hadn't he thought of that? "Well?" he asked.

"You're right, some did, but I'll have to check my bank for details," Machin said.

"Don't worry, we'll get the information ourselves. We'll get a warrant to access your bank accounts," Calladine said.

"Taking liberties, that is. What if I object?"

"Why would you?" Ruth asked. "You've nothing to hide."

Machin didn't look happy. He grabbed the mop off Calladine and turned his back on them, muttering while he worked. "Is that it?" he asked finally. "Only I want to get set up for opening time."

"That's all for now, we'll leave you in peace." Calladine smiled. "We'll see you again, no doubt."

Once they were outside, Calladine said. "Good call of yours, the card thing. I must be slipping — it didn't even cross my mind."

"You've got a lot to think about with Eve being missing."

Calladine sighed. Didn't he just, not least of it having her family on his back for the duration. They'd expect him to have all the answers when, in fact, he didn't have a clue.

CHAPTER 29

"Have you met any members of the Buckley family before?" Stephen Greco asked.

Rocco shook his head. "Even DI Calladine doesn't see that much of them."

"Is there bad blood between them all?"

Rocco didn't know how much Greco knew about Calladine's personal life, so he was reluctant to say more. "Not that I'm aware of, sir."

"They're a wealthy family. That firm of theirs employs a lot of people."

"You're thinking Eve Buckley is the perfect target?"

Greco looked at the young DC. "I'm not sure. Given that DI Calladine's a member of that family, this could be more personal."

Rocco was hoping the DCI would elaborate, but he didn't. They'd parked the car and were walking towards the office block. Simon Buckley came out to meet them.

"Have you found her?"

Greco shook his head. "Not yet. Can we talk to the staff, please, particularly the young woman who was with your mother when the ransomware email was opened?"

"Wendy? Yes, of course." Simon led the way down a corridor and into a large office overlooking the hills at the back of the building. "Mum liked this office, she said the view was much better than looking out over the industrial estate." He gestured to a young woman sitting at a desk. "This is Wendy."

Greco sat down. "We're here about Mrs Buckley. You were with her when the attack happened. Will you talk us through what happened?"

Wendy put the sugary doughnut she'd been eating on the desk, smiling broadly at Rocco. "She was checking the emails. There were loads, and Mrs Buckley was working her way through them. She saw one she reckoned was urgent and should be actioned right away. It was an amended order from Haywards. She opened the PDF attachment and all hell let loose. All the office computers locked up. Mrs Buckley was shocked, she couldn't believe it. Nothing would work. When she got over the shock and realised what had happened, she rang Colin, our IT person."

Greco nodded at the doughnut. "Shouldn't you put that on a plate? It'll leave the surface sticky and get all over the paperwork."

Rocco stifled a snigger. He'd heard about Greco's ways. Had he actually listened to her, he wondered, or had he been too concerned about the sticky table? Rocco was curious to see the girl's reaction. She chose to ignore the comment.

Greco turned to Simon Buckley. "Tell me about Haywards."

"They're a string of chemist's shops and they get a large amount of their stock from us. They're good customers."

"Who would know that?" Greco asked.

"Obviously we do at Buckley's, but our customers are not a secret. Anyone can find who they are."

Greco turned back to Wendy. "The order. Did you see it?"

The girl shuffled through a pile of paperwork. "I have a similar order from them, but I can't find it right now."

Greco shook his head.

"I was looking over Mrs Buckley's shoulder at the order with the ransomware as it appeared on screen, but it looked fine," she went on, "just like all their others."

"What about the email it was attached to? Who it was from, that sort of thing."

"Mrs Buckley didn't seem to see anything suspicious about it."

"That's right. Mum told me that it looked exactly like all the others from Haywards."

"Okay, thank you, that was helpful."

Simon Buckley looked at Greco. "What will you do next?"

"We will visit Haywards' main office and speak to them. Whoever the culprit is must have known a great deal about how the company operates."

Back in the car, Greco took a wet wipe from a pack in the glove compartment and cleaned his hands. "There's no way I could spend time in that office. There was sugar residue all over the surfaces and the carpet was covered with crumbs."

* * *

Calladine and Ruth decided to visit Roxy at the Duggan. She'd been looking at Ramsey's mobile, and if there was anything useful on it, they needed to know urgently.

"Sorry this has taken a while. I was tied up with the ransomware thing. The service providers will email you the call log. I'll look at his browsing history, the emails and all that next, I promise." She smiled.

"We're short on both evidence and leads in this case, Roxy. Anything you get, let me know at once."

"Ruth!" It was Rob.

She smiled at him. "I thought you weren't in today."

"I had an early dental appointment." He looked at the mobile in Roxy's hands. "Do you want me to take a look?"

"This one is down to digital forensics, and that means me," she said. "If I don't find anything, you can give it the onceover."

"Whose is it?" Rob asked.

"It belonged to Kieron Ramsey," Ruth said. "It's the one found at his flat."

"I'm still working on the lad's clothing. If I get anything, I'll be in touch straight away."

"We are desperate, Rob," Calladine said.

Roxy held up the phone. "And if there is anything on this little baby that you can use, I'll find it and let you know at once."

"That's one of the reasons I enjoy working here, everyone is so good at what they do," Rob said.

Ruth and Rob strolled towards the corridor. "So, you do enjoy working here after all," she whispered. "Only last night you gave me the impression that you wanted something else."

"A little hasty of me, perhaps. I'm fine here for now." He smiled. "Want to go out again?"

Ruth nodded. She'd like that very much.

* * *

Calladine and Ruth arrived back at the station to find Alice alone in the main office.

"Rocco is with DCI Greco," she told them. "They've gone to Buckley's."

Greco was welcome to that part of the investigation, and to Simon. Half-brother or not, Calladine felt uncomfortable around the man. There was a conversation they'd never had. It hung in the air between them but Calladine didn't want to push it. "Anything come in while we've been gone?"

"No, sir."

Calladine handed her a note. "I want you to get onto this bank. I need the records for card payments made at Holme Internet Café for the last three months. Tell them a warrant is being obtained."

He turned to Ruth. "Would you organise that? Tell the magistrate it's urgent. I don't want to give Machin time to hide anything."

"He can hardly hide his bank transactions — stop being so paranoid."

Calladine had hoped that there would be more from Julian, but they'd just come from the Duggan and there'd been no sign of him. They had a body and two missing women, and no one in the frame. He was about to retire to his office with a mug of tea when a uniformed officer hurried into the room.

"A body has been found, sir, up at Doveclough Lake. Some bloke rang it in five minutes ago."

So much for quiet reflection. "Get hold of Natasha and Julian, will you, Ruth? Tell them to meet us up there." Calladine turned to the constable. "Do we know anything else?"

"Only that the bloke who found it was fishing. He saw a shape bobbing in the water, looked at it through his binoculars and realised it could be a body. He didn't explore further, instead he called us. He's still in shock."

"Poor bloke, was he up there on his own?"

"Yes, all he wanted was a quiet day fishing."

"There's carp in that lake, some big ones too. I used to fish it myself when I was a lad." He saw the look Ruth gave him. "What's so odd — me being a lad or the bit about fishing?"

"Looking at the state of you now, both, to be frank."

"You're getting worse, Sergeant Bayliss. No respect, that's your problem."

"Who's driving?" Ruth asked. "I doubt my little car will get us up that steep track."

"I'll drive and we'll take a pool car, a four-track job."

"Who do you think it is?" she asked.

"I know who I hope it isn't," Calladine said.

CHAPTER 30

Doveclough Lake was situated high in the hills above Leesdon. It was surrounded by tracks used by walkers, but there was only one access lane. Natasha Barrington, Julian and Rob had arrived before Calladine and Ruth. The body had been lifted from the lake and was laid out on the grass beside the water. It was wrapped in fabric from head to toe and taped up tight. It was impossible to tell if it was male or female, never mind identify it.

On seeing it, Calladine gasped. Ruth grabbed his arm. "It won't be Eve."

But that wasn't it. What shocked him was that he'd seen a body done up like this before. "It'll have been weighted down with stones," he said. "And that fabric will be an old curtain." He released Ruth's grip. "And you're wrong, it could be Eve." His voice shook with emotion. Despite his vast experience, he wasn't sure if he'd be able to stand here and watch this.

"Let's hope it's not her," Ruth said gently. "You can sit in the car if you'd rather. I can do this on my own."

"No, I have to know. I need all the information I can get. If it does turn out to be Eve, Greco will have me off the case in a flash."

The two detectives watched while Natasha Barrington carefully cut the fabric away from the body's face.

"Female," she shouted to them.

"Oh God. It's her, isn't it?" Calladine turned and walked away, and Ruth heard him throwing up in the long grass.

"He needs to know if it's Eve, his mum," Ruth explained.

"She has blonde curly hair if that helps," Natasha told her.

Ruth spun round. "Not Eve!" she shouted. "This one's a blonde."

Calladine wasn't sure how he felt — relieved of course, but also horrified at that relief. But if this wasn't his mother, then who was it?

Knowing full well what would be going through his head, she said, "My guess is that it's Moira Haigh."

"I think you're right," Rob said. "I saw a photo of the woman when we were at her house."

"What did you mean, you've seen a body like this before?" Ruth asked.

"I've seen photos, Ruth," Calladine said. "The murder Machin did time for. The photos showed all the preparations the killer made before disposal, the curtain, stones and the tape. And the one here is exactly what the body looked like in those pictures."

Natasha had removed the fabric from the head and torso. "We'll do the rest back at the Duggan. She's naked and the upper body and face is badly bruised. She took quite a beating."

Ruth shuddered. "Poor woman."

"Exactly like the Machin killing." Calladine moved closer so he could watch as Natasha examined the woman's mouth.

"She's had her tongue removed, Tom, just like Ramsey."

That was an aspect Calladine had no idea about. From the images he'd seen of the previous murder, there was no way of telling if it was the same MO. But what was done to Ramsey had not been released to the press or anyone outside the team. "The same killer?"

"I'll get her back to the lab before I commit. But it's looking that way," Natasha said.

Calladine's mind was racing. There was a huge difference between Kieron Ramsey and Moira Haigh. But there were links between them. Gina for one — Moira's niece was known to both of them. And the internet café was another. The ransomware had been in an email sent from there, and Ramsey frequented the place.

And then there was Clifford Machin.

"We will do a thorough search of this area," Rob said. "Although I doubt she met her end here."

"Dump site, then. No doubt the killer hoped she'd never be found," Calladine said.

"But for a spot of bad luck it would have worked too," Rob said. "The fisherman over there spotted a shape in the water. He saw it clearer through his binoculars. Realising what he'd found he called the police. It took a boat and two men to haul her to the side."

"I want divers in the lake," Calladine suddenly announced.

"Why?" Rob asked. "Your mother?"

Calladine nodded at the water. "Possibly, but I have a hunch that the body of one Jimmy Merrill might be in there. He's an old case, body never found. There are strong similarities in how the bodies were prepared and left." He looked at the young fisherman who was standing nearby, shaking, a blanket wrapped around him. "He's in a state. Get his details and we'll speak to him later."

A uniformed officer spoke up. "His name is Stuart Sykes, sir. He lives in Leesdon. I've got his address." He passed it to Calladine.

"Thanks," he said and, turning to Natasha, he asked, "When will you do the PM?"

Natasha Barrington thought for a moment. "It's getting late. I'll do it first thing tomorrow. Will you get a relative to do the identification?"

Calladine nodded. "Text me the time."

"We off now?" Ruth asked.

"I need a word with Greco. He has to find Eve before she ends up like Moira. They were both targeted by ransomware and neither paid up."

"That doesn't mean Eve will be killed," Ruth said.

"Oh yes it does. One way or another, this maniac is determined that his victims will pay. If not in bitcoin, then with their lives."

"You don't think this is personal, do you — you being Eve's son?" Ruth asked.

"I'm beginning to think that's possible. But if you're going to hold a computer system to ransom in Leesworth, then Buckley's is an obvious choice. They are successful, well known and have money."

Ruth nodded. "We'll have to tell Gina about her aunt. Want me to do that?"

"Yes, she will have to do the ID, and see if she's got anything else to tell us. This will shock her, make her realise what her aunt was dealing with."

"Do you think this has anything to do with Noah Ash — the drugs or Holme Internet Café?"

"Well, there are several connections, not least the name 'Snowdrop.' And Machin, but that's a puzzle I haven't solved yet."

They went back to their vehicle and were out on the main road when Ruth's mobile rang. It was Alice and she sounded excited.

"Dr Atkins has been on the phone. She tried to reach your mobile, but you must have been out of range up at Doveclough. She's found some photos on Ramsey's mobile."

"What sort of photos?" Ruth asked.

"Of Noah Ash. It looks like he visited that internet café too — and got himself into bother."

"We'll be back shortly. Print them out, would you?"

CHAPTER 31

Alice laid the photos out on Ruth's desk for her and Calladine to look at. They showed Ash having what looked like a row with Clifford Machin at the internet café. In the first one, Machin was holding Noah Ash by the scruff of his neck.

"Ramsey must have taken the images in quick succession, sir. Look, in the last one Machin is throwing Ash out the front door."

So, Machin had lied. He did know Ash, but why were they arguing?

"I want to interview Noah Ash again," Calladine told Alice. "Would you find out if he's up to it? Ring him but keep it friendly. We've nothing on him at this point, so we want his help, that's all."

"Worried he'll throw another sickie?" Ruth asked.

"He was genuinely ill. I had no idea the lad was asthmatic."

"The attack will have been brought on by anxiety. He'll have been worried about what you had on him," Ruth said. "What about Machin? He'll need interviewing again."

"Leave Machin to me."

Alice put the phone down. "Noah is at home, recuperating. His mother said he spent the night in Leesdon Infirmary.

She didn't sound happy, said it was all our fault. But he has agreed to speak to us, provided we go to him."

That was okay with Calladine. "Ruth, you can drive. I need to think."

"About Eve?" she asked.

"Yes, but more pressing is working out what the relationship is between Noah Ash and Machin."

"Machin fixes computers, perhaps that's it."

"We're not aware that Ash has any interest in computers. And there are umpteen firms in Oldston and the surrounding area that do computer repairs if that was his problem. No, Ruth, Ash visits Machin for a different purpose." Calladine picked up the photos Alice had given him.

"Greco is alone in his office," Ruth said.

"I'm not up to talking to him. My patience is wearing thin. If he had any information about Eve, I'm sure he'd come and tell me."

"D'you want me to ask him?" Ruth said.

"I'm not scared of the man, Ruth, just wary of losing it with him."

"Come on then, let's get Noah Ash sorted and go from there."

Calladine and Ruth left the station and made for Ash's house in Hopecross. As they pulled up in the lane, they saw two uniformed officers standing by Eve's front gate.

"Too bloody late," Calladine muttered.

"Perhaps if Eve had said something when the attack happened . . ." Ruth said.

Ignoring her, Calladine said, "We have to catch this bastard, Ruth. I hope that Rob of yours is up to the job. We need all the forensics we can get."

"Rob is excellent at what he does, even Julian says so. Give him a break, Tom."

"Seeing him again, are you?"

"Probably. I like him."

* * *

130

Noah Ash's mother was waiting at the front door. She took them through to the conservatory, where Noah was watching TV.

"He's refusing to take his tablets," his mother complained. "I told the doctor he was rubbish at taking his medication regularly."

"You should take them," Calladine said to Ash. "Asthma can be serious."

Ash gave them a filthy look. "Yeah, that last attack might have been fatal, thanks to you."

Calladine tried to be conciliatory. "We're not here to upset you, Noah. We simply want to ask a couple of questions."

"Sit down. I'll get some tea," Ash's mother said.

Calladine smiled. "Not for us, thanks. We won't be long."

"Okay, if you want me I'll be in the front garden."

He turned to Noah. "Have you ever visited Holme Internet Café in Huddersfield?"

Ash shook his head. "Why would I do that? There are at least three computers in this house."

"Do you know someone called Clifford Machin?"

"Never heard of him."

That was a blatant lie, but why was he denying it? "In that case, how d'you explain this?" Calladine handed over the photo of Noah and Machin.

"That's not me, mate. And I've no idea who that is," he said, pointing at Machin.

"We have more photos, Noah," Ruth told him. "You're lying. You have been to that café and you do know Machin."

"There's no way I'll admit that. I'm not telling you anything else either. If you want to speak to me again, I'm having Falkner with me. You should leave now. I'm not up to this."

"What does Machin have on you, Noah? Is it the drugs?"

"What drugs? I've no idea what you're talking about."

"You, Kieron Ramsey and a man known to us as Snowdrop all used that internet café. Tell me what went on there."

Ash shrugged. "Haven't a clue. You've got the wrong bloke. I know Ramsey from the asthma clinic, but the others — no idea who they are."

"Did you ever talk to Ramsey when you were at the clinic?" asked Ruth.

"You do know that Ramsey was murdered? As yet, we haven't found his killer. Unless you want to become our prime suspect, I suggest you tell us what you know," added Calladine.

"I've told you, I know nothing."

"Okay, forget Ramsey. It's your relationship with Machin I'm really interested in," said Calladine.

"Can't help you there."

"Is he supplying you with the drugs you peddle?" Calladine asked.

"Not guilty. You've got the wrong bloke." Noah Ash got to his feet. "Now get out of my home and stop pestering me. I don't know anything, and I can't help you. I'm not the man you want."

"Okay, but we will talk again," Calladine promised. "And when we do, I will have the evidence to charge you."

"What with? Visiting an internet café? You've got to be having a laugh."

CHAPTER 32

As Ruth and Calladine made their way back in the car, they saw Noah's mother pottering about in the garden.

"Hang on, I want a quick word." Ruth said.

Mrs Potter was busy dead-heading in the flower border. "Lovely garden," Ruth said, as they approached. "Bet it takes some keeping up."

Mrs Ash smiled. "The garden is why we bought the house. I love it out here and the view of the hills is beautiful."

Ruth nodded. "You're very lucky. The girl who was here the other day, the one my colleagues spoke to, d'you know much about her?"

"Not really, just that she's a friend of Noah's. Alina, I think her name is."

"Does she visit often?"

"I don't know. Noah has another part of the house separate from me. I don't watch his every move."

"Do you speak to her much?" Ruth asked.

"Alina doesn't have very good English. But, yes, sometimes we chat — not about anything in particular, just general things."

"Where does she come from?" Ruth asked.

Mrs Ash stiffened. "Why are you asking all these questions about Alina? What do you think she's done? First you harass my son, and now this innocent girl." She pointed to the gate. "I want you to leave now."

Ruth returned to the car.

"What was that about?" Calladine asked.

"I'm curious about the young woman you and Rocco saw the last time you were here, that's all."

Calladine shrugged. "She looked harmless enough to me."

"We should take nothing and no one at face value," Ruth said.

"You're right. I want Ash watched," Calladine said. "When we get back, I'll organise surveillance." He cast a look towards Eve's house.

"Why not call in, have a word with Simon?" Ruth suggested.

"And say what? I'd only be giving him false hope. For all we know, Eve could turn up dead tomorrow."

"What about Machin?" Ruth said. "He lied too. You showed him a photo of Ash and he said he didn't know him."

"I've missed something," Calladine said. "You get off home, see to that boy of yours. I'll stay at the office and go over what we've got."

"What d'you expect to find?" she asked.

"I don't know, but I have to do something."

They drove back in silence. While Ruth drove, Calladine scrutinised the photos from Ramsey's mobile. Ruth glanced at him. This case was getting to him in a way that she'd not seen in a while. He was concerned about Eve, which was natural, but there was something else. Ruth had a shrewd idea that it was Machin. She wondered if Tom was afraid of the villain.

As they pulled into the station car park, Ruth asked, "What now?"

"I've got a couple of jobs to see to."

"Want a hand?"

"You could ring the family liaison person who's looking after Gina and ask them to bring the girl to the morgue tomorrow morning to ID her aunt. I'll sort getting Ash watched."

"You should get off home yourself, take Amy out for a drink perhaps. You need some down time, Tom. The case is wearing you out."

"Don't worry about me, I'll be fine."

* * *

Fifteen minutes later, as Ruth pulled onto her drive, her mobile rang. It was Rob.

"Fancy something to eat?"

Ruth smiled. Not having to cook sounded wonderful, but she couldn't keep imposing on Anna. She had been looking after Harry since the morning and would have had enough.

"I have to see to my son, Rob. I've been out all day and need to be home."

"Perhaps I could come round, bring something with me? I'll get us a takeout from the restaurant we went to the other night."

"If you don't mind the mess, and me in my PJs, that's fine with me."

She heard him laugh. "See you in an hour — and I'll bring some wine."

Food problem sorted, Ruth went inside. Rob was shaping up nicely. Jake was welcome to his new life. If that's what he wanted, stuff him — it was about time she had some fun.

CHAPTER 33

Tom Calladine didn't want to go home. He knew he wouldn't sleep. His mind was too full of the case. His time was better spent going over everything they'd got so far. The main office was quiet and at this time of the day there were few phone calls to distract him, the perfect conditions in which to work and think. He pored over all the statements, scoured the forensic reports and looked again at the photographs they had, including those of Moira Haigh's body lying at the side of Doveclough Lake.

After an hour or so, he'd reached the only possible conclusion. It was as Ruth had said — slap bang in the middle of this case sat Clifford Machin.

The man would have to be brought in, but Calladine's stomach churned at the thought. Greco would argue the point, so would Quaid. They'd question whether his interest in Machin was personal, obsessive even, tell him to leave it to another officer, but he couldn't do that. He and Machin had history, and because of that, in some twisted way they understood each other. If anyone was to tackle the man with the evidence they'd got, it had to be him.

A further thirty minutes passed before Calladine grabbed his jacket, his keys and a bottle of single malt he kept in his desk drawer and left for the night. But he wasn't going home. No, he was going to have an off-the-record chat with Machin.

Everything they had pointed to the villain, but all of it was circumstantial. Machin must figure in this somewhere. At the very least, it had to be him organising the drug dealing and using Noah Ash to distribute it in Leesworth. But was he responsible for the ransomware demands and the killing of Ramsey and Moira Haigh? It was a possibility. The man had done time for murder.

* * *

"I hope I'm not disturbing you," Rob said. "You work long hours — I didn't think."

Ruth smiled, ushering him inside. "I invited you round, idiot! And anyway, you've brought food, so you're more than welcome."

He held two bottles aloft. "And wine — one white, one red."

Ruth took the bag containing the food through to the kitchen, Rob following her. She retrieved the plates that had been warming. "You got more of that delicious pasta we had the other night, perfect." She smiled. "Have you just finished work too? The job's great but the late shifts can be a killer. I'm well aware that when we're up against it, so are you folks at the Duggan. On more than one occasion, Julian has gone at it all night."

Rob opened the bottle of red and poured two glasses. "He works hard, that's for sure."

They sat on the sofa in Ruth's sitting room, with the food on their knees.

"How are you getting on with Julian?" she asked.

"He doesn't say much, and as for a sense of humour, I don't think he has one."

Ruth laughed. "You've got his measure, alright. Poor Julian is a straight-faced workaholic who prefers his own company. There has only ever been one person who could reach him, and that was Imogen."

"Natasha mentioned her. She was killed, I believe."

"Yes, and her death was devastating for Julian. But we look out for him. He's as much one of us as anyone."

Rob was looking at a photo on Ruth's windowsill. It showed Ruth, Jake and Harry, taken in happier times. "Is that your partner?"

Ruth took a swig of her wine and shook her head. "Ex-partner," she said. "His choice. He dumped me in favour of someone else."

"You don't seem too bothered, if you don't mind me saying."

She smiled. "You have softened the blow."

He gave her a peck on the cheek. "Only too pleased to help."

"We were struggling, to be honest. We tried very hard to make things work, mostly for Harry's sake. But we were on a downward spiral. I'll probably look back and see Jake going like that as a good thing for both of us."

"What about the house, your living arrangements?"

"It's a problem, because half of it belongs to Jake," she said. "He will provide for Harry, but he has to live somewhere and if he buys another place, he'll need his share of this one."

They were interrupted by a knock on the front door. "Excuse me, I'll see who it is and get rid of them." She got up and went into the hallway.

Ruth opened the door to see Jake standing there, swaying. He was drunk. "Want to talk," he slurred. "We should. I've not treated you right and I'm sorry."

Ruth pushed him away. "Not now, Jake. Come back when you're sober. What happened? Orla throw you out, did she?"

But Jake tried to grab her arm. "It shouldn't end like this. Let me in, please."

"I've got company, now bugger off. You made the decision to split, so live with it. I'm not interested in your excuses, Jake," Ruth said.

At that moment, Rob appeared and stood behind her.

"I see. Didn't take you long to find a replacement, did it?" Jake stumbled backwards and fell into the drive. "Okay, I'll leave you to it. You're a right bitch, Ruth, but you know that. And as for you," he pointed at Rob, "don't get too comfy, because all she thinks about is that bloody work of hers."

Jake staggered off down the road.

"I'm sorry, Ruth. I should go. You need time to think things through. Perhaps we should leave this for a while," Rob said.

"No way. I'll see whoever I like whenever I want," she smiled, "and that includes you. Sod Jake Ireson. That man no longer has anything to do with my life. It was his choice, not mine. We will both have to live with it."

CHAPTER 34

Clifford Machin stood blocking the doorway. "This is twice now you've bothered me today. What the hell d'you want this time?"

"A word."

Clifford Machin stood aside. Calladine brushed past him into the café. "You're lucky," Machin said. "I was about to lock up and bugger off home."

"Where d'you live?" Calladine asked.

"In the flat upstairs."

Calladine moved a PC to one side, took a seat and put the whisky bottle on the desktop. "Got a couple of glasses, Cliff?"

Machin picked up the bottle and inspected the label. "Good stuff, a single malt from that distillery in the Highlands Fallon was so fond of. But then you'd know that."

"Not really. We didn't socialise."

Machin got two glasses from behind the counter and sat down facing Calladine. "C'mon then, what's this about? You've not come here for a drinking session. What you after?"

"Answers, Cliff. And I know you've got some of them."

Machin poured himself a large whisky and downed it in one. "I did not kill Jimmy Merrill! How many times, Calladine?"

"We've got another one, done up in exactly the same way. Odd coincidence that, given you're out and we've had nothing like it in all the time you were away."

"Not down to me. No way!"

"Well you can't blame Fallon this time, he's long gone."

"He said you were the bright one, but I think he was wrong on that score. You're like a stuck record, Calladine. I've told you before, and I'll keep on saying it until it sinks into that thick skull of yours. Fallon set me up, planted evidence, then sat back and watched me take the rap. You know what he was like — you grew up with him, for God's sake."

"We found the latest body in Doveclough Lake," Calladine said.

"A favourite of Ray's, that place. Fished it often enough. You too, as I remember."

Calladine poured them more whisky. "This place — make much, does it?"

"Enough to keep me in fags and pay the rent."

"Computer Science. Where did that come from?"

"Some whiz kid I met inside reckoned there was a fortune to be made in designing apps, you know, those things on mobiles. I signed up for the course, but I couldn't get the hang of it. I got a reasonable qualification though. When I got out, this place came up — more my level."

"D'you know anything about ransomware?" Calladine asked.

"It's a bloody pain in the arse if you get targeted, I know that much."

"Would you know how to target someone?"

"What is this? What d'you think I've done?"

Calladine took the photos of the bust-up between Machin and Ash from his pocket. "Know him, do you?"

Machin took a good look and then shook his head. "Just another troublemaker I had to show the door to. Why? What's he to you?"

"He pedals drugs in Leesworth. Someone is supplying him, and he's told us that someone is you, Cliff," Calladine lied.

Machin laughed out loud. "Where would I get the stuff from, Calladine? I don't have the right contacts any more. I'm old hat, long forgotten. The movers and shakers in the drugs business these days wouldn't give me a look-in."

"I think those movers and shakers use this place as a drop-off point. They drop, you mind the stuff for a while and Noah Ash comes by and picks it up. He's described to us in detail how it works. You might as well come clean."

Would he fall for it? Calladine waited. He needed the information Machin could give him.

Machin wrapped two hands around the glass. "Perhaps you're the bright one of the bunch after all. Okay, I admit, I mind the stuff until that idiot picks it up."

Calladine tapped the image of Noah Ash. "This idiot in the photo? You admit to him coming here?"

"Well, I've got my hands round his neck there, so I can hardly deny it, can I?"

"I have asked you about him before and you lied, said you'd never seen him."

"What can I say? Lying, getting involved with drugs, I'm a bad boy," Machin joked.

"Does he know anyone else here?" Calladine asked.

"I've no idea. I don't think so. Occasionally he talks to some of the punters, but mostly he just picks up the stuff and goes. Whatever he's pedalling is hidden in a laptop bag. Make a tidy sum, the amount you can stash in one of them."

"And it's regular?"

"Yes. Every few days."

"Who drops the stuff off?"

"I don't know her name. It's always early and I sleep late. You'll have to have a word with Nathan." He checked his mobile. "Look, is this important? Because I'm really missing my bed. It's been a long day and now I'm pissing around with you. And let's face it, Calladine, I can think of plenty of other people I'd rather be pissing around with."

"The drop-offs are made by a woman?" Calladine asked.

"Yes."

"I could arrest you, Cliff. You've broken the conditions of your licence."

"Fair comment, but what actual proof d'you have? Just the word of some young scally."

"You needn't worry, Cliff. I won't make any of this official and as far as I'm concerned, this little catch-up never happened. But there's more to this than just the drugs. My mother has been kidnapped."

Machin gave him a quizzical look. "I thought Jean died a while ago."

"She did, but it turns out she wasn't my real mother. Eve Buckley — ever heard of her?"

Machin shook his head. "Sorry, can't help you there. You can search the place if you want, but I can promise you, I didn't take her."

"I've got two bodies, one kidnap, and two systems targeted by ransomware, and this place is at the centre of it all. Why is that, Cliff?"

Clifford Machin laughed again. "In some respects, I envy you, Calladine. There's never a dull moment in your life. Best of luck with all of that, but I know nothing about the killings or the kidnap. And, I should point out that if any of these murders were recent, I'm stuck in here day in, day out. You know that, you've been in my face often enough recently."

"The Jimmy Merrill murder — did Ray ever talk about it?"

Machin stared at Calladine long and hard. "Said the kid had squealed a lot."

"He beat him first?"

Machin nodded.

"Anything else?"

"The lad was a grass. He knew the risks. If there was one thing Ray couldn't abide, it was folk telling tales. And he had a pretty effective way of dealing with them."

"Murder," Calladine said.

"Eventually, yes. But he was a cruel bastard. He hated the lad for what he did. Ray lost a small fortune because Merrill snitched to you lot."

Calladine had a bad feeling about what was coming next. "What did Ray do to him?"

"Before he finished the lad, he cut out his tongue and stuffed it down his throat."

CHAPTER 35

Day 6

First thing the next morning, Calladine got a text from Natasha telling him the PM would be at eleven. Despite it being the weekend, he and the team were still hard at it. He drove to the station in reflective mood. He was actually beginning to consider that Machin might be telling the truth, and it had been Ray Fallon who'd killed Merrill. But Machin had admitted to handling the drugs, so there was still a niggle of doubt at the back of his mind. Machin was clever, and the fact that Moira Haigh had suffered the same fate as Merrill was one hell of a coincidence.

"I rang you last night and got no reply," Ruth said. "Did you go out?"

"Yep," Calladine said.

He wasn't ready to discuss his chat with Machin yet, not even with Ruth.

"Amy or Emma?" she asked.

"Neither. I had a quiet pint on my own in the Wheatsheaf," he lied.

"My evening wasn't much better either. Rob came round, brought food, some wine, and just as we were getting cosy, Jake turned up drunk and made a scene. Rob felt guilty, so he left."

"Lucky escape," he joked, and then became serious. "You need to be careful. I mean, what do you really know about the man?"

"I don't know where that attitude of yours comes from. Rob is a great bloke, he's one of the Duggan team, and like it or not, we will have to rely on him if we want results."

Calladine pulled a face. Was it simply that Rob Harris was new, or were his instincts telling him something? He'd attempted to jump into Jake's shoes quick enough, perhaps that was it. "Natasha wants us at eleven. Does Gina realise what we're asking of her?"

"Yes, the Family Liaison Officer has explained the procedure. I'm meeting them both at ten. Gina will do the ID and return to the safe house."

"How did she take the news?" Calladine asked.

"According to the FLO, she barely looked up from her phone. Some kids are heartless, I don't understand it myself."

Calladine disappeared into his office with a mug of tea. He'd slept fitfully and was tired. Too much whisky and a head full of Machin meant he'd tossed and turned all night. The most notable snippet the man had let fall was that Jimmy Merrill had had his tongue cut out. Why would Machin tell him that if he was guilty of killing Moira Haigh?

He checked the timescale. Machin was right. Moira had been taken during the daytime while Machin was working at the internet café. His young helper Nathan would no doubt provide an alibi should one be needed. Just in case, Calladine decided to get Machin's phone records. Given the drugs involvement, they were worth a look.

"You ready?" Ruth asked from the doorway. "Are you up to this, Tom? Only you look weird."

"Thanks for that. I'm worried sick — Eve, remember. For all I know she could be breathing her last right this minute. She doesn't deserve that, Ruth. I've let her down."

146

Ruth stepped into the office and closed the door behind her. "Let's get one thing straight. You couldn't have known that this would happen. We're working flat out trying to find the killer. He will slip up, Tom, they all do. We will find Eve, you have to keep strong."

He threw her his car keys. "The Duggan. Will you drive?"

"I can do this alone if you're not up to it," she said.

He took a last swig of the tea. "Get some fluids down me and I'll be fine."

"Heavy night, eh? Thought you said pint, singular."

"Half a bottle of single malt is more the mark, and in the worst company possible."

"Who?"

"Clifford Machin."

* * *

Ruth drove fast. Calladine sat silently, offering no explanations. Within minutes, they were pulling into the Duggan car park.

"I'll go and meet Gina," Ruth said. "Why don't you find Julian? Get him to make you more tea or something."

Ruth strode off, leaving him behind. She was losing patience. He'd spent time alone with Machin — not a wise move, and he should know better. She understood the pressure Calladine was under, but bullying Machin into submission was not the answer. If Machin decided to, he could make a heap of trouble for Calladine.

Gina Haigh was waiting with the Family Liaison Officer, a woman called Sonia, who Ruth had met before.

"Are you okay with this?" Ruth asked Gina. "You don't have to be afraid. Your aunt will look much as you remember her." Ruth was hoping the absence of a tongue would not be obvious.

The girl shrugged, tore her eyes from her mobile and stuffed it in her jeans pocket. "Can we just get on with it?"

Ruth smiled at her and led the way to the viewing room. A technician was waiting for them at the door. "Do you want to look through the window?" Ruth asked.

"I don't mind, I'll go inside if you like, make sure it's her."

She seemed utterly devoid of emotion. Ruth was sure it had to be some sort of act. She ushered the girl inside the room, and the technician gently pulled the white sheet from Moira's face.

"Yes, it's her. That's my Aunt Moira."

Gina turned on her heel and went back into the corridor. Seconds later, she was on her mobile to Arron Cookson.

"She's well and truly dead," she told him. "She only had me, so that house of hers must be mine now." She looked at Sonia. "D'you know if my aunt made a will, and where I'll find it?"

Ruth was shocked. The girl's heartless attitude made her feel uncomfortable. Gina wasn't in the least bit upset about her aunt's death. All she was concerned about was the inheritance.

"I'll leave you two. We'll speak later," Ruth told Sonia.

Ruth made her way to the morgue. Never a pleasant place, but the experience she'd just had with Gina Haigh had left a bad taste in her mouth.

"You okay? You look a little pale." It was Rob.

"I'm fine — odd experience with a relative of Moira Haigh's. Not what I expected, that's all."

"Did you sort out last night's problem?" he asked.

"Yes, all's fine now. I'll ring you later," she said.

CHAPTER 36

Rocco was alone in the office when the phone records came through from Arron Cookson's provider. He printed out the list and started to wade through it. Most of the calls were from Gina's number, but there were others too. One had rung him half a dozen times up until the previous week. Rocco wondered if that could be Noah Ash.

"Bingo! I think our burner phone user has to be Noah Ash. The only calls to and from the phone are Gina and one other number."

"And you think that's Ash?" asked Alice.

"Yes, has to be. It's about time Noah answered our questions properly and stopped mucking us about."

"But you can't prove it's Ash's phone, not unless you find it," Alice said.

"When's the boss back?" Rocco asked her.

"Him and Ruth have gone to the Duggan for Moira Haigh's PM," she said.

Someone was calling from the doorway. "Can I help, Simon?"

It was so rare that anyone at work ever called him by his real name that it took him a moment or two to respond.

It was Greco. "Sorry, sir, but would you mind calling me Rocco? The only person who calls me Simon is my mum."

Greco nodded, his expression unchanged. Rocco couldn't tell if the super approved or not. "I overheard your conversation," Greco said. "Is it your intention to speak to Ash again?"

"I'd like to know if this number belongs to a phone he owns."

"Find out if he's still at home recuperating and we'll go together," Greco said.

Once he'd left the office, Rocco pulled a face. "He's not easy to get along with. In fact, he's damned hard work. I went with him to Buckley's yesterday, and he spent the whole journey back going on about the state of the place."

"I think he's okay," Alice said. "A little odd in his ways, but there's nothing wrong with that."

Alice was too understanding, that was her problem. As far as Rocco was concerned, Calladine was right about the man. He rang the Ash house to be told that Noah was still convalescing. He warned Noah's mother that he and DCI Greco would be visiting later that morning.

Rocco was about to go to Greco's office and tell him when Greco himself appeared. "Where's Calladine?" he demanded.

"At the Duggan, attending a PM."

"In that case, we can't wait. We must go to the Buckleys' house right away. There's been an incident."

So much for speaking to Ash. Rocco grabbed his jacket and hurried after Greco. "What sort of incident, sir?"

"Mark Buckley, Simon's son and Eve's grandson, has been kidnapped. His dad reckons he was taken some time earlier this morning while he was out jogging. They have received a text message, demanding money."

* * *

"She has the same pattern of bruising and cutting as Kieron Ramsey," Natasha said. "Moira put up a fight. She also has bruising to her knuckles, and her fingertips and nails look as if they've been burnt." Natasha took a swab. "I think he tried to destroy any forensic traces. If she'd scratched him, it would have left residue under her fingernails. There is regular demarcation, as if he dipped her fingers in acid."

Ruth shuddered. "That poor woman, fighting for her life."

"What killed her?" Calladine asked.

Natasha made some incisions, revealing the back of her throat. "Same as with Ramsey — tongue cut out and pushed down her throat. She died of asphyxiation, but not immediately. She will have choked on the blood — in effect, slowly drowning — and once the tongue was pushed in there, death would have followed."

"The fabric she was wrapped in, has that given you anything?" Calladine asked.

"Julian and Rob are on it. The stones used to weigh her down are nothing special, just the type you find in abundance up on the hills around here. Black duct tape was used to bind the fabric, effectively making the body a secure parcel for disposal."

"Killed at the site?" he asked.

"Julian says not. Taken there and dumped. Have a word with him before you leave. He's running toxicology tests and working with what we've got."

But was it enough to give them that much-needed lead to the killer? Calladine strode off towards Julian's lab. He wanted a quiet word.

Julian Batho shook his head as Calladine walked in. "You know it's far too soon for me to have anything useful for you."

"I am desperate, Julian. The bastard has taken Eve. If I don't find him soon, she's going to end up like Moira Haigh."

"I understand, but my first findings are very general. The killer is forensically aware. He has done a number of things to make things as difficult as possible for us. The acid burns to her fingers, not leaving her clothing behind and dumping her in the lake. But he didn't intend her to stay hidden for long. The stones he weighted her down with were not sufficient to ensure the body remained on the bottom. Once the body began to decay, it would float to the surface. Everything he used in her disposal is freely available. The fabric is commonly used to make curtains and cushions and can be got in many shops. However, I did find the remnants of a price tag in one corner. It was handwritten, so it is just possible that this particular fabric was from a set of curtains bought from a charity shop. I've sent you a photo of the design. The tape is standard and there are no prints on it."

"We've got nothing, then." Calladine turned and hurried off, leaving Julian to his work.

Ruth called to him from the corridor. "Tom! I need to speak to you."

"What now?"

"There's been a development. Mark, Simon's son, has disappeared. He left for his run at about nine this morning and didn't return. Simon has received a text demanding money for his and Eve's return. It's from the people who were responsible for the ransomware."

CHAPTER 37

Calladine hadn't expected this. For a moment he didn't know what to do. He wanted to find them, make them safe, but where to start?

"I have instructions from Greco to make sure you return to the station straight away. He's speaking to your family now," Ruth said.

"I should go and join them. Simon will expect me to do something."

"Greco says no, and he doesn't want you going rogue either," she said.

That was all very well, but he couldn't just sit around the office doing nothing. Calladine followed Ruth back to the car. "I'll drop you. There's something I want to do."

Ruth wasn't happy. "Greco expects you to do as he says. He is the DCI. The boss, in other words. Your choice, remember?"

"Never mind all that. I'm not going near the Buckleys, just following a hunch. If Greco asks, I've gone to see Zoe."

"He'll see right through that one. Come on, what's on your mind?"

"Leave it, Ruth, I know what I'm doing. Anyway, it's better you don't know in case it backfires."

"And there was me thinking we were a team."

"Don't start, Ruth, I'm not up to arguing the toss right now."

Calladine dropped Ruth at the station and drove off. First Eve and now Mark. This had got personal very fast, and in Calladine's opinion that pointed to one person — Machin.

He parked up outside the internet café and was surprised to see the place locked up. There was a note on the door to say it was closed due to illness. Or had Machin simply done a runner? The villain could be behind the ransomware, the dealing and the murders. Calladine kicked himself for not acting sooner. Machin should have been brought in straight away.

A voice shouted to him from an upstairs window a couple of doors down. "If you're looking for Cliff, he's not there, he's had a fall. Nathan has taken him to A & E."

"Bad, was it?" Calladine asked.

"Bad enough. He might have broken a leg. Howled the place down, he did. Took them paramedics ages to calm him."

"Huddersfield A & E?"

"Yes. I imagine he'll be needing surgery."

* * *

Ruth returned to the incident room to find an excited Rocco. "I've found something. The info came in for the phones belonging to Ramsey and Cookson. There was nothing of interest on Ramsey's, but Cookson only sent and received calls from two numbers. One is Gina's, and I reckon the other has to belong to Ash."

"But we can't be sure?" Ruth said.

"We know Cookson dealt drugs for Ash. Who else would he be ringing?"

"We need to find the burner used by Ash to be certain of that. And then we want the one that was used to send the texts to Moira Haigh and Eve Buckley when they were targeted," Ruth said.

"You think the cases are connected?"

"We simply don't know. But that internet café links them both, and that has to be more than just coincidence. Still, it's a start. Very well done, Rocco. We'll bring Noah Ash in again and confront him with what we've got. He is now our most promising lead to whoever is behind the drug dealing."

"I've tried ringing the burner phone, but it's dead." Rocco said.

"Where's the boss gone?" Alice asked.

"Officially, to see his daughter, Zoe. Unofficially, I've no idea. When he heard about Mark, he took off and wouldn't tell me where to."

Rocco pulled a face. "Greco won't like it if he doesn't toe the line."

"Not Calladine's style, though, is it? He's obviously got some theory rattling around inside his head. Just wish he'd told me what it was."

The office phone rang. It was Julian. "Is Tom there?"

"No, and I don't know when he'll be back either."

"I've texted him but got no reply. We've found something on the tape used to bind Moira Haigh's body. I wanted to discuss it with him."

"Will I do?" Ruth asked.

"Let me do further work first. But if you speak to him, tell him it looks promising."

It wasn't like Julian to be so coy. "Are the initial forensics in from the Haigh murder?" Ruth asked Alice.

Alice checked the inbox. "Yes, notably an image of some curtain fabric, from a pair thought to have been bought from a charity shop or somewhere like that."

"Would you visit the local ones, Alice, see if anyone recognises it."

"It's a long shot. It could have come from a jumble sale, a car boot, or the killer could have been given them," Alice said.

Ruth shook her head. "We're running out of time. Let's keep it simple for now, and ask in the town first."

"I've sent a couple of uniforms to bring Noah Ash in," Rocco said. "Perhaps now he'll believe we mean business. It'll certainly give him and his mother something to think about."

CHAPTER 38

Calladine had a quick scout around the A & E waiting room but there was no sign of Machin.

"They've taken him to X-ray," someone called. It was Nathan.

Calladine sat down next to the lad. "What happened?"

"He was cleaning the café window and fell off the ladder. He went down like a ton of bricks, must have fallen ten feet. He's hurt his leg badly and banged his head."

Calladine studied the hospital guide. X-ray was on the first floor. "I'll see if I can find him."

Leaving Nathan, he took the lift and followed the signs. Machin was in a wheelchair, waiting in a queue with three others. Calladine sat down beside him.

"Bloody fool, what were you doing up a ladder? You should have got Nathan to sort the windows."

"I'm not in the mood. What d'you want now?"

"Injured or not, Cliff, we need to talk. Things don't add up. You haven't been honest with me."

"I can't help you. For starters they've given me a hefty dose of morphine. You're wasting your time talking to me. Anyway, I know nowt. All this about murder and drugs. Someone is playing you, me too probably."

"Tell me about Jimmy Merrill."

"I didn't kill him."

"But you do know more than you said at the trial. If you're innocent like you say you are, why do that?"

"I value my life," he said. "I'm no different from anyone else on that score. Ray might have been a friend but cross him and he could become a deadly enemy."

"But you and Ray were close."

"Out of necessity, and because of the jobs we did. Bottom line, your cousin was a murdering scumbag. He enjoyed killing, revelled in making people suffer. He even took photographs, for pity's sake."

"Jimmy Merrill?"

"Exactly. The lad crossed him, big deal. He deserved a thumping, nothing more. What he got was way over the top. Ray couldn't help himself, he was in a rage and lost it."

"And you took the blame. Why?"

"He threatened me. I'd seen the full extent of what he was capable of with Merrill. I had no choice. Ray sweetened things a bit by paying me. That's how I managed to buy the internet café when I got out. I stashed the money in an account under a different name. Ray said if I told anyone what really happened, locked up or not, he'd finish me."

Calladine didn't know what to make of this. "Do you have any evidence, Cliff?"

"No. But I know where you might get some. Look at those photos of Merrill. Have them blown up if you have to. They were taken inside Fallon's garage, that's where he did Merrill. You can see Marilyn's dog paintings in the background."

He was talking about Sam, the dog Calladine had adopted when Marilyn had gone to prison. Calladine knew Ray couldn't abide that dog of hers. Hence, his wife had to paint her portraits of Sam away from the house. "Do you know where Merrill is?"

"Yes. He's at the bottom of the lake near that fancy house of Ray's. The one where he used to windsurf."

"Lowmere?"

"That's the one."

"Can you think of anyone who'd want to set you up?"

"Oh, plenty. I've been inside, I made enemies. And then there are the people I pissed off years ago. And how d'you know it's me they're setting up? This could be down to someone wanting to get at you."

"Whoever it is knows details about the current killings that we haven't released yet," Calladine said.

Machin grunted. "Naked, beaten, tongue cut out and body taped up in fabric. The finishing touch, weighted down and dumped in water."

"Spot on." Calladine shook his head. "You know a lot about these killings, Cliff, and I'm beginning to think it's because it's you who are guilty."

"Well, I'm not. Look at me. It's all I can do to get through the day and remain standing. I'm not strong enough to go hauling dead bodies about, and most of the time I'm drugged up to the eyeballs."

"Why?"

"Because I'm running on empty. I've got chronic heart failure — look at my bloody ankles." He held up his good leg. The lower half was swollen and red. "It's only the drugs that are keeping me going. Do anything too strenuous and I keel over. I fell off that bloody ladder because I had a dizzy spell."

"What time did you fall?"

"Ten past nine this morning. I smashed my watch when I hit the pavement."

"Mr Machin?"

They looked towards the young doctor who'd called Machin's name.

"I'm afraid you've broken your right femur and it will need pinning to fix it."

"I have to stay in?" Machin asked.

"Yes indeed. You'll have surgery in the morning and then you're going to need physio."

"Sorry, Cliff," Calladine said. "Looks like you'll be laid up for a while. I'll tell Nathan. Is he able to keep the café going?"

"Yes, if you don't piss him off. I need him to keep the place open, so bear it in mind."

Calladine left Machin to the tender care of the nurses and went to find Nathan.

"Your boss will be laid up for a while. Think you'll cope?"

"No probs, I'll get a mate to help me."

"Tell me about the drug drops, Nathan."

The lad looked at Calladine, his eyes wide in fear. "Machin said it would be okay, that no one would find out."

"Well, I have, and I want answers. The name of the person who delivers the stuff to the café will do for starters. Machin reckons it's a woman, always early, and mostly it's you on duty at that time."

"To begin with I'd no idea what it was. Just a laptop case to pass on, but they kept on coming, regular, several times a week."

Calladine was losing patience. "Who, Nathan?"

"A girl — young, pretty, and with a foreign accent. I don't know her name. We never got that far. She just dumps the case, collects the cash and scarpers."

"We'll talk again. I want a description, and you will help one of my people create an identikit image."

CHAPTER 39

By the time Calladine arrived back at the station, it was gone five. He could do with going home, calling it a day, but there was still a lot to do.

"We're bringing Noah Ash in again," Ruth told him. "Rocco has found some evidence regarding the burner phone we're interested in."

"Good, I need a word with that young man myself. Where's Alice?"

"Having a wander around Leesworth's charity shops, trying to find where those curtains came from. And you? Where have you been all this time?"

He laughed. "Holding Machin's hand. The man fell off a ladder and broke his leg. He's going to be laid up for some time."

"Did he ring you?"

"No. I wanted a word, but when I got there he was already in A & E."

"At least we'll know where he is and what he's up to." She gave him one of her looks. "A word about what? Are you still hounding the man?"

"I'm still not certain, but I think he might be telling the truth. Machin can't have taken Mark this morning, he was being carted off in an ambulance."

"He could have got someone else to do it. And what about the murder he was convicted of?"

"He told me that was down to Ray. Mind you, he's been saying that for years." He thought for a moment. If Machin was right, there was no point in continuing the search up at Doveclough. "I need a word with Greco." Calladine needed to know if he had anything on Eve and Mark's disappearance before he called off the search.

* * *

Stephen Greco was at his desk. "From what I can gather, Mark Buckley was taken at some point during his morning run. When he didn't return, his dad rang him and got no answer. The lad had left his mobile at home. Minutes later, Simon Buckley got the text demanding a ransom and we swung into action."

In that case this was definitely not down to Machin. The timescale didn't fit. "The text — do we have the sender's number?"

"It's in your brother's statement, which is on the system."

"Good. And Simon is my *half-brother*," Calladine said. "I still haven't got used to being related to the Buckley family, and to be honest, I doubt I ever will."

"It's a fact, there is no getting away from it. And whether you are close to them or not, you can't investigate their disappearance," said Greco.

"I know that. I'm busy looking at other aspects of the case." Calladine said. "There is a lake in Cheshire called Lowmere, and I have been given information that the body of Jimmy Merrill was dumped there. This was twenty years ago but the Merrill case has strong links to the killing of Moira Haigh."

"You want this lake searched?"

"I think it would be wise. Even after all this time, there may be useful forensic evidence."

"A man was charged with that murder — Clifford Machin. Have you been in contact with him?" Greco asked.

Calladine wasn't going to lie. Whether it got him in trouble or not, Greco should know the truth. "Yes, we've chatted several times during the last few days. Machin's internet café figures prominently in the investigation, so I have had little choice."

"Is he involved?"

"I'm not sure."

"Okay, but don't talk to him again without telling me. Machin might be out on licence, but he's still a dangerous bastard."

* * *

"This isn't funny any more. I'm fed up of being dragged in here," Noah Ash said.

Calladine smiled. "Apologies, Noah, but it can't be helped. You haven't been honest with us, and until you are, you will be staying here."

Ash looked at his solicitor. "Can they do this? Isn't there something you can do to stop them? This lot are doing my head in."

Calladine showed him the burner phone number they believed belonged to him. "Do you own the phone with this number?"

Ash looked at the figures on the scrap of paper and shook his head. "Not mine, sorry."

"I think you're lying. This is your phone, isn't it? You used it exclusively to call Cookson and your boss."

Ash shook his head. "Haven't got a clue what you're on about."

"You're lying, Noah. You've had several calls from this number. I think it's the one you use to organise the drugs drops at the café."

"No comment."

"You see, the problem we've got is that the internet café was used to set up two people — Kieron Ramsey and Moira Haigh. They're both dead, murdered in cold blood."

Ash turned pale. "No comment. I'm not saying another word."

"That's your choice, Noah. But I would advise you to tell me what you've done with the burner phone."

"You can't prove it's mine."

That was true. "No, but what we can do is search your home. Think we'll find it, Noah?"

"My mother won't like it."

"We've further investigating to do and until we're finished, you will be our guest," Calladine said. "I doubt your mother will like that much either."

Ash turned to Falkner. "Sort this! I can't stay here, I've got things to do. Get me bail."

The solicitor shook his head. "Noah, I would advise you to be truthful, tell them what you know."

The young man slammed his fist onto the table. "Why won't anyone listen! I haven't done anything. This is all rubbish."

Calladine was sick of hearing Noah Ash protesting his innocence when the fact was, he was in it up to his neck. His plan was to wear Ash down until he gave up the information about who he was working with.

"We'll resume in the morning. Get a good night's sleep, Noah. You're going to need it."

CHAPTER 40

On Calladine's return to the office, Ruth collared him. "Julian rang you earlier. He wouldn't tell me much, he wants to speak to you, says he might have something."

"I'll phone him shortly."

"Are you okay? You're looking tired again," she said.

"We get this little lot sorted and I'll be fine. For now, there's no chance of me relaxing while Eve and her grandson are still missing."

Ruth sighed. He was right. "Want to eat at mine? I'll cook. I'm doing nothing else. A quiet night in, just me and Harry, and once the little man's in bed, a bottle of wine."

Calladine gave her a smile. "Thanks, but I'd be lousy company. No, you get off."

He looked at Rocco, who was also getting ready to leave. "Do we have any photos of Ash's car during the search?"

"I'm not sure. I would think so."

Calladine picked up the office phone and rang Julian. "You wanted a word?"

"I have been examining the tape used to bind Moira Haigh's body. Stuck on the glue I found a human hair. It isn't hers, Tom. I'm working on the theory that it might belong to the killer and I'm testing for DNA."

If Julian's theory was right, that was brilliant news. "I hope it gives us something, Julian, we certainly need it. You searched Noah Ash's car during his last spell in custody?"

"We found nothing, Tom, other than a bag of groceries."

"Did you take photos?"

"Of course."

"Would you text them to me?"

"For what purpose?"

"Just following my instincts, Julian."

Within minutes, Calladine's mobile pinged with the texts. He opened each one and looked carefully at the images.

Rocco had his jacket on, ready to go home. Calladine passed him his phone. "What d'you see?"

"I presume it's the boot of Ash's car. All that's there is a supermarket carrier bag."

Calladine then showed him the print of Noah Ash in the café, alongside the one in the text. "And remember, these were taken on the same day."

"I don't know what I'm looking for," Rocco said. "Give me a clue."

"It's about something I was told earlier today. In the café photo, the one where Machin is about to throw him out, Ash is carrying a laptop bag, one of those cloth padded things. But it's not in the car boot or inside the car. Ask yourself, where did it go?"

Rocco looked confused. "Is it important?"

"Very." He took out his mobile and called Julian again. "Julian, I'm sending a party out to do a search of the area where Ash's car was found. He reported it stolen, but I suspect that was a cover because he knew he'd been spotted making a drugs drop on the Hobfield."

"What are you looking for, Tom?"

"A laptop bag, or the remnants of one. If we get lucky, would you process the findings straight away?"

"As you wish."

Rocco had already put his briefcase back on his desk. "You'll be needing a hand. I can show you where Ash was parked and where the kids congregate."

"Thanks, Rocco. I'll organise some uniforms and we'll get this done."

* * *

Two hours later, an exhausted but jubilant Calladine delivered the tattered pieces of a laptop case to the Duggan. "Found in a rubbish bin." He grimaced. "You can see how the inner padding has been cut out. Done, I suspect, so that more drugs could be stuffed inside."

"Your instincts could be correct," Julian said. "I'll run tests and get the results back to you pronto. I'm primarily looking for drugs, but there will be DNA on the outside. The case is fabric, not leather, and a host of debris will have stuck to it."

That was music to Calladine's ears. "I'll be in touch tomorrow. I've got the young thug it belonged to in custody. With your results, I'm hoping to throw the book at him." He was about to leave it at that, when something occurred to him. "Do me a favour, Julian, when you're running any tests to do with this case, would you check them against the DNA of one Clifford Machin? He's an ex-con, so he should be on the database."

"You think he's involved?"

"No, but it would ease my mind to know for sure." Calladine looked at Julian. He was as tired as him. "No Rob to help you?"

"He had a heavy date. I presume with Ruth — the two of them seem to have become very pally of late."

Ruth hadn't said anything. She'd told Calladine it was a night at home for her. "Are you sure he's seeing Ruth?"

"No, not really. Rob doesn't discuss his private life with me, but I know they have seen other recently. He might not say much, but he did mention how much he liked her. Is it important?"

"No, not really. I'm just curious. How d'you find him?"

"He's good, dedicated to the work but difficult to talk to. I tend to leave him to it. I can't pin it down, but I find him odd in some way."

Calladine smiled. Julian was one of the most introverted people he knew. He and Rob ought to have a lot in common, so why didn't they get along?"

"Have you discussed him with Amy?" Calladine asked.

"She's met him. She came to pick me up one night earlier in the week. She disliked him at once. Said he had a bad aura, and that he was not what he appeared to be."

"You do know that stuff is rubbish, Julian? Rob is new. He's finding his feet. You have quite a reputation, you know. That takes some dealing with. He is working in your shadow, poor man."

CHAPTER 41

Day 7

"Gran? Are you okay?" Mark Buckley called out.

Mark strained his ears to hear. He was blindfolded and couldn't see a thing, but he knew she was somewhere close because he'd heard her groan and try to call out. He could also hear water trickling somewhere nearby. His other senses told him that he was underground. He had caving experience and the smell was the same, moss on wet stones. His clothing was wet too. Wherever he was lying was sodden.

"Gran! Speak to me if you're there."

Mark's hands were tied behind his back. He sat up and shuffled forward, feeling with his feet for his grandmother.

"I feel strange," she whispered.

"You're somewhere nearby but I can't see you. Are you able to sit up?"

"I'm too dizzy. Where are we?"

"I've no idea, Gran, but we need to get out of here fast. That man will come back and who knows what he's got planned for us."

"I can't remember what happened," she said.

"We've been kidnapped. He took me on the lane while I was out for a run. But you've been here longer than me. Has he given you anything to drink?"

"No, and my mouth is as dry as a bone."

"We've been drugged. Don't worry, they'll find us." Mark touched his gran with his foot. She was lying down just in front of him. "I need you to sit up," he said. "If we sit back to back, we might be able to untie our hands."

There was no reply. Eve Buckley had slipped into unconsciousness again.

"Gran!" he shouted. "You have to help me."

He heard her moan. Whatever they'd been given must have affected his gran much more than him. Mark realised she wasn't going to be much help. He drew up his knees in front of him. He had to find a way to prise the blindfold from his face. It felt like a rag of some sort. After rubbing at it with his knees for several minutes, the thing slipped to his chin.

It didn't take Mark's eyes long to become accustomed to the gloom. He was right, it was a cave of some sort. There were pipes running down the wall at one end. "Gran!" he called. "Please wake up."

There was no response. Eve was out of it. "They'll find us, Gran. You must hang on." He shuffled forward and nudged her gently. "When he jumped me there was a scuffle. I fell over, but I managed to stuff my smartwatch down my sock. He hasn't found it. It has GPS enabled. Dad will realise and send help."

* * *

"This is becoming a habit," Calladine said. "I reckon you want us to stop questioning you as much as I do. Am I right, Noah?"

Noah Ash glowered at him. "I'm saying nothing. I've got rights. I don't have to talk to you."

"That's right, but it will help you if you tell me the truth. And it could stop you from being charged as an accessory to murder."

Calladine doubted the lad was involved in the killings of Kieron and Moira, but he needed a lever to get him to talk. He let the little snippet sink in. It had its effect. Ash looked wildly around the room until his gaze settled on Falkner.

"Tell him! That was a threat! He can't say things like that. I've not killed anyone."

"You own a mobile?" Calladine asked.

"Nothing wrong with that, most people do."

"Yes, Noah, but I'm interested in the one you keep hidden. The pay-as-you-go, the one you change regularly."

"Rubbish. You're making it up."

"No, I promise you I'm not. I've got proof."

Calladine was silent. After a few minutes, he showed Ash an image on his own mobile. "Your home was searched yesterday evening, and we found the phone hidden in the toilet cistern of your en suite bathroom. Want to tell me who gave it to you?"

"Okay, I use it sometimes to ring friends, that's all. My mum can't keep her hands off my contract one and there are things I don't want her to read, you know, texts to the girlfriend and that."

"Now it's you spouting rubbish, Noah. You used your burner phone to contact Cookson and one other person, that's all. What did you talk about?"

"I can't remember."

"You and this unnamed contact of yours must have been pretty pally. Where did you meet? That internet café in Huddersfield? Was it the girl who did the drop-offs? Want to tell me her name? Things might go easier for you if you help us."

"It's not worth it. I value my life." Ash tapped the photo. "Anyway, I don't know the place, you've made a mistake there."

Calladine put another photo down on the table. It was the one showing Machin throwing him out. "Explain that, then."

Ash said nothing.

"Interesting fact about this photo," Calladine said. "You're carrying a laptop bag. But look at this one." He showed Ash the image of the boot of his car. "Just groceries, like you said, but no laptop case. What happened to it?"

"How should I know?"

"No matter, we've found it. Pieces of that case are being analysed in our lab as we speak. What's the betting our forensics people find traces of drugs along with your DNA?"

Noah Ash grabbed his solicitor by the jacket lapels. "You've got to stop this! Do something! This is all wrong!"

"All wrong, is it, Noah? Then tell me the truth," Calladine said.

"I was told this wouldn't happen. They said things had been put in place so I wouldn't be arrested. And anyway, that there was no evidence to convict me if I was."

"Whoever told you that was lying. You've been had." Calladine waited for a response. The lad seemed confused. "Whoever is running the drugs operation will let you take the blame for the lot — the drugs, and possibly the ransomware demands. And the murders. They all lead back to that café. Now, let's try this again. Who were you working for? Who told you to pick up the drugs?"

Noah Ash sat back, as if resigned to his fate. He'd obviously reached the end of the line, and realised lying was no longer an option. "It was all done by mobile, and I was given a new one regularly. We never spoke, it was always a text. I went to the internet café, picked up the laptop case. The drugs were in it."

"You took the drugs to the Hobfield. That was your patch?" Calladine asked.

"Yes, I distributed through Cooksie. He knew the users and collected a lot of the money."

"What happened to the money?"

"I kept my cut but most of it went back to the café."

"Who dealt with you at the café?" Calladine asked.

"Mostly it was Nathan, but sometimes the old man."

Now they were getting somewhere. "Thanks, Noah. See, that didn't hurt, did it?"

CHAPTER 42

Noah Ash would be charged. Calladine returned to the incident room, where Ruth collared him.

"Julian wants you. Said it was urgent," Ruth said.

Calladine smiled. "I got a confession from Ash. Now Julian has come through on the forensics. Things are looking up."

"Ring him first. You don't know if he's got something or not yet."

But Calladine could feel it. He was close. Although what he really wanted was to find Eve and Mark.

"What have you got? D'you know where they are?" he asked when Julian answered.

"Not yet, but that hair found on the tape around Moira Haigh's body? Well, we do have a DNA match on the database," Julian said.

"Go on, I can't stand the suspense."

"Clifford Machin."

Calladine realised he'd been had. Machin had conned him, almost had him believing in his innocence. How bloody stupid was that? All that guff the man had spouted was nothing but lies. "You sure?"

"Absolutely, there is no doubt. Also, traces of heroin were found in the laptop case along with Noah Ash's DNA. However, we also found DNA belonging to another individual — not on the system, I'm afraid."

"Probably the drop-off person. I hoping to get a lead on her shortly."

"There is something else. The curtain fabric Moira Haigh was wrapped in. Remember we thought she might have attacked her killer? Well, I found a faint trace of blood, not hers, and not matching any DNA we've collected so far."

"Not Machin's? Not even a match to the unidentified DNA on the laptop case?"

"No, Tom."

Calladine would have to give this some thought, but for now he had more important things on his mind. They had the murders and the ransomware, but the drugs case appeared to be separate. Yet all the cases were linked to Machin's café, which was odd. Calladine did not believe this was just a coincidence. "I'm going out," he told Ruth.

"Want company?"

Given the mood he was in, that wasn't such a bad idea. Right now, Calladine could happily have throttled Machin for lying to him. "Okay, but be warned, we'll be going to see Machin in hospital, and then we're bringing in Nathan from the café."

"Machin? Why? If this has anything to do with your mother Greco won't like it."

"Stuff Greco. Machin is a lying toe-rag and he isn't getting away with it."

"I think you'd better calm down." Ruth snatched the car keys from him. "I'll drive and you can tell me what's happened to upset you so much."

"Before you go, sir." It was Alice. "I've been round all the local charity shops and none of them recognise that curtain fabric."

"It's okay, Alice. I think they came from somewhere else."

"Where, sir?"

"I reckon it must be near Machin's internet café. Give it an hour, and then organise a search of that place, top to bottom."

"What are we looking for?" asked Rocco.

"Burner phones and anything else that doesn't fit."

"Want to tell me what's happened to make you so angry?" Ruth asked as they made their way down to the car park.

"Clifford Machin. That man is everywhere. Julian has found one of his hairs on the tape used on Moira Haigh's body."

"That's it then, you have your man."

* * *

Calladine searched the board in the hospital entrance for the orthopaedics department.

"First floor, next to X-ray," Ruth said. "We'll take the lift."

Calladine said nothing, he was desperately trying to calm himself down. He might be bloody angry at Machin for having fooled him, but despite being officially off the case, he still needed the man's help to find Eve and Mark.

"I know what you're thinking," Ruth said, "but you won't get anywhere coming across all heavy. Kid gloves, Calladine. He's had a big op. Be nice and you might get what you want."

"You must be joking. If he doesn't tell me what I want to know, he'll be lucky to keep his teeth."

There was only one ward in orthopaedics with a dozen beds in it. Calladine could see at once that Machin wasn't there. He went to the nursing sister's station and asked for him.

"Mr Machin is in our intensive care unit on the first floor," she said. "Are you a relative?"

"An old friend," Calladine lied.

Ruth tugged him away. "We'll go there and find out what happened," she whispered. "There's only so much she can tell you — patient confidentiality and all that."

"What d'you reckon's happened to him?"

"It could be anything. He's not a youngster, perhaps the anaesthetic didn't agree with him."

"I need answers, Ruth. Eve and Mark are in real danger."

They took the stairs down to the first floor. The doors to ITU were locked.

"You can't just walk in and out. There are very sick people in there," Ruth explained.

A nurse approached them. "Can I help?"

Calladine showed her his badge. He wasn't having any more excuses, he needed to speak to Machin. "Clifford Machin. I need a word."

She shook her head. "Not possible, I'm afraid."

He thrust his badge into her face. "This says it is."

"You don't understand, Inspector. Mr Machin has had a massive stroke. He's not expected to regain consciousness."

CHAPTER 43

DCI Stephen Greco received an urgent call from the Buckley household. Simon Buckley admitted he was close to losing it. He needed to know what they were doing about his missing family. Greco decided he'd pay him a visit, have a talk to the man and try to calm him down. He took Alice Bolshaw with him. During his short time with the team at Leesdon, Greco had found her very promising. The young woman had a future.

They arrived to find Simon pacing around anxiously. "My mother and son are out there somewhere. You haven't found them yet and I haven't a clue where to start looking. I have no choice but to pay up."

"That is never a good idea," Greco said.

"I'm all out of good ideas," Simon retorted. "I need to make sure they're safe."

"Did Mark have his phone with him?" Alice asked.

"No, he left it here. He wears his smartwatch when he's running."

"Some of them have GPS," she said. "Did Mark's?"

"Yes, it was all singing, all dancing, you can even ring it. That's it!" Simon yelled. "That's how we'll find them. I should have realised, but what with the worry and lack of sleep my mind is so shot, I'd forgotten about that."

"We might be lucky, providing Mark still has it on him," Greco said. "I'll make a call. We'll get our IT forensic experts to locate Mark." Greco went into the hallway and rang the Duggan. It was Roxy Atkins he wanted but Rob Harris who answered. "Mark Buckley was wearing a smartwatch when he was taken," he began. "It has GPS. I want that watch located and a search organised. Pass this on to Dr Atkins urgently. When you have a position, ring me back."

Next, Greco called the station. "I want people on standby for a possible rescue," he told Rocco. "The lad was wearing a smartwatch, so with luck we should have the location of Mark and Eve Buckley shortly."

* * *

Within half an hour, Rob rang Greco back. "They're up in the hills, near that lake where the body was found. Always provided the lad still has his watch with him."

"We'll keep our fingers crossed," Greco said.

"Doveclough Lake," he whispered to Alice. "And that was a good call you made regarding the GPS."

"We're wasting time, we should leave. Every minute is vital," said Simon.

"Slow down, Mr Buckley. We'll leave it to the experts."

"I know the hills around here as well as anyone. I will not be sidelined," Simon insisted.

"No one is doing that, but I want you to remain here with DC Bolshaw. I will ring periodically, and she will keep you up to date with events."

* * *

"Do you have enough against Machin to be sure that he's our man?" asked Ruth.

"He knew all about Moira Haigh's body, what was done to her, how it was left, and we found his DNA on the tape.

He admitted to being involved with the drugs, and the ransomware came from his business property. Yes, I think we have enough," Calladine said.

"We've done it then. Greco finds Eve and Mark and it's case sorted. All you have to do now is prepare a file for the CPS."

"Case sorted providing Greco finds them safe and well," he reminded.

"*Almost* over then," Ruth agreed. "But if anyone can find them, Greco can."

But Calladine still looked miserable. "Cheer up," she nudged him. "This is shaping up as another success. You should be pleased with yourself. Good work all round."

All she got in reply was a grunt.

Calladine attempted a smile but it didn't quite work. "No, you're right, it's a good outcome."

Ruth sighed. "Want to tell your face that? For someone who's just solved two particularly nasty murders, you don't look happy at all."

Calladine was checking his mobile. "Greco's got a lead on Eve and Mark. He might know where they are."

"Even better. We just have to hope they are both okay. Greco finds them and it really is celebration time."

The look on Calladine's face hadn't changed. Something was bothering him.

"Speak to me, Tom. Tell me what's wrong."

"Nothing, not really, but it doesn't feel right. Not logical I know, but I've got these doubts circling in my head. I'm not absolutely sure about Machin. Yes, he told me things about Moira Haigh's body, but he was likening it to what Ray did to Jimmy Merrill. He wasn't talking about his own actions. I know he acted as a drop-off point for the drugs, but that doesn't make him guilty of murder, or the rest."

"If not Machin, then who? And how did his hair get on that tape? You're not making sense, Tom." Ruth was fast becoming annoyed with him. "There is no one else in the frame — not Ash, not Cookson, no one. Machin is our man. And he will have done all of it to get back at you. He hates you, you said as much. That man has waited years for the chance to put you through it. Well, it's over, and you need to get a grip."

CHAPTER 44

"Help!" Mark Buckley screamed. "We're in here." He could hear voices outside somewhere, but they sounded a long way off. "Gran, they've found us, it's going to be okay."

But Eve Buckley didn't stir. Mark was worried. He'd got little out of her apart from the odd moan, and she'd hardly moved at all.

"In here, we're in the dark!" he shouted.

Suddenly he saw a light, hovering around the cave walls. It moved in their direction.

"Mark?"

"Yes, we're over here, but my gran's in a bad way. You have to help her first."

Two men wearing caving gear with torches on their hard hats came towards him.

"It's okay, son. There's an ambulance outside, we'll soon have your gran on her way to hospital."

"We're tied up. She's still wearing a blindfold. Be careful, don't shine the light in her face."

The man said nothing to Mark, but he could see that the woman was very sick. She was cold and unresponsive. "Come on, Mark. Let's get you out first and then I'll get a stretcher in here for your gran."

Mark Buckley was led carefully outside, across the floor of a huge cave-like expanse and through a heavy iron-clad door.

"Belongs to the water board," the man explained. "Gives the operatives access to the piping running from the reservoir."

"I need to tell my dad we're okay."

Someone called to him. "I've already told him. I'm DCI Greco, I work with your uncle. Good job you had that smartwatch on you. Otherwise—"

"I fought with him," Mark said. "I scratched his arm. While he was hopping about in pain, I hid my watch down my sock."

"Good thinking."

"I want to see Tom. I need a word," Mark said.

"About what happened? You should not discuss that with him. You are family, that's why this part of the case has been handed over to me."

"I just want a quick word. A phone call, that's all. The battery on my smartwatch will be drained by now."

Greco nodded and handed him his mobile. Mark walked a little way off to be out of earshot.

"Tom, it's Mark. We're out, and safe. Gran is on her way to hospital, she's not right."

"How bad is she?" Calladine asked.

"I don't know. She's cold and out of it. Didn't say a word all the time we were in there."

"I'll meet her at the hospital."

"Before you go, there's something else. I scratched the kidnapper, and I've got his blood on my T-shirt."

"Brilliant, Mark. Give it to DCI Greco, he'll get it to our forensics people. In fact, let me speak to him."

Mark passed the phone back.

"The lad has blood on his clothing belonging to whoever took him. Will you ensure that it gets to Julian?"

"I'll take Mark to the Duggan myself. Julian will take what he needs and then I'll get him to the hospital."

"I'll meet you there."

* * *

"Good news?" Ruth asked.

"The best. Greco's found them. Mark sounds fine but Eve is poorly. I need to get to Leesdon Infirmary, check on them," Calladine said.

"I'll drive," Ruth said. "You sit and chill — and try telling yourself that this is finally over."

"Machin didn't take Eve or Mark. He must have had help."

"Leave it to Greco, that's his part of this investigation. You said yourself how many villains Machin knows. He'll have roped in someone from his murky past to do the job."

"You could be right," Calladine said. "And if that's so, we will get him because we've got his DNA. Mark scratched the bastard. If he's a villain, it'll be on record."

"No need to stress then. But let Greco do his job. He is capable, you know."

Calladine shook his head. "This case is tricky. It's not what it seems and that bothers me."

"Rubbish. Things are exactly what they seem. Machin is guilty and he had help, no doubt about that — probably that Nathan who works with him."

"No, not him. He's not strong enough. He's a skinny lad and short, he couldn't take on our Mark and win. Mark works out, he's a big man, and tall," Calladine said.

"We're going to interview him anyway, so we'll see."

CHAPTER 45

Eve Buckley was in the High Dependency Unit. She had mild hypothermia and had reacted badly to whatever drug the kidnapper had given her.

"She might look grim, but the doctor says she'll be fine," Simon told Calladine. "She's been lucky. Had it taken any longer to find them, things could have been very different."

Calladine was hugely relieved that Eve and Mark were back and safe. If this had indeed been down to Machin, he was now incapacitated, so Calladine presumed there had been no opportunity to murder them. Still, they could have remained in that underground space, undiscovered, for a long time.

"Greco says you know who's behind it," said Simon.

"Yes. The main suspect is currently in hospital, at death's door, so he's no longer a threat."

"That means you won't get the opportunity to speak to him?" Simon asked.

That had been bugging Calladine. There were still things about this case that he wasn't happy with. Another chat with Machin had been on the cards.

"I'll leave you to it," Calladine said. "I'll keep you informed of events. Your Mark's a good lad. Quick thinking, knew his clothing was important. Given the scuffle he had with the kidnapper and the fact the bloke had bled, he knew there'd be DNA on it."

"He has ambitions to join the force." Simon Buckley shook his head. "Nothing to do with me. I've tried to put him off, but the lad is set on the idea."

Calladine nodded. Why not? "Encourage him — he could do worse."

He left Simon to it. He still felt uncomfortable around the Buckleys. He'd been catapulted into their life in middle age and he would never fit in — not an ideal situation for either party.

Ruth was waiting for him in the canteen. "C'mon then, give me a smile. I know she's going to be fine, I've been talking to the doc."

Dr Sebastian Hoyle had been the team's pathologist before the entire facility was transferred to the Duggan. Now he worked part-time as a locum at Leesdon Infirmary.

Calladine smiled. He'd not seen the doc in a while. "Is he okay?"

"Yep, fine. He asked about you. I told him you were your usual moody self. What's up now, for goodness' sake? You've still got that face on."

"Just that lot upstairs — the Buckleys. I still can't get used to having this 'pop-up' family all of a sudden. Not just Eve or Samantha — now there's Simon and his son Mark. Mark wants to be a copper, by the way."

"Good choice. Perhaps he's inherited a stray gene. You must have got your enthusiasm for the job from somewhere."

"I'll drop you back at the station, then I want a word with Julian. I need to discuss one or two things."

"What about Nathan? Is he still important?"

"Yes, he's going to provide a likeness of a young woman I want to speak to. But I'll deal with him later."

* * *

Julian was alone in his lab when Calladine turned up.

"Did you get Mark's T-shirt?" Calladine asked.

"We have all their outer clothing and will check for any DNA that doesn't belong to them, Mark's top included," Julian said.

That wasn't good enough. Calladine had to ensure that this was done properly and in his book, that meant Julian. "Would you make a point of doing that particular item yourself?"

Julian swung round and stared at his friend. "Is something wrong, Tom? You appear to have developed trust issues all of a sudden."

"Definitely not with you, Julian. I can't explain how I feel, but, please, indulge me this one time. It could turn out to be very important."

Julian didn't look too happy, but he agreed. "As you wish. I'll be in touch the minute the results are known. Do you want to discuss anything else? Your reasons, for example?"

Calladine shook his head. He had no idea himself why he wanted things like this. It was down to pure instinct, not solid information. But he couldn't rid himself of the notion that something was very wrong, and he'd missed it.

"Before you leave, you should know that Rocco dropped off a mobile with Roxy earlier. She is looking at it now."

That would be the one belonging to Noah Ash. "Thanks, Julian. Speak later."

Calladine strode down the corridor towards Roxy's lab. She was hard at it, head bent over a screenful of information.

"Quite a lad, your villain. Got all the chat, kept his little gang on a tight leash. Look at these." She swung the screen round so Calladine could read the text messages. "Meet-ups, strict instructions on what to do. I wouldn't want to cross this one."

"You should meet him. Soft as butter. That's all talk, believe me. Who were the texts from?"

"Only two numbers rang this phone. One we know is the burner belonging to Arron Cookson, and one is unknown."

Calladine groaned. "Yes, I know that from the phone records. There's another one out there that we haven't found yet. It could belong to whoever picked up the drugs at the café." He thought again of the mysterious young woman he'd seen at Noah Ash's house. "Do any of the texts sent to the unknown number suggest that it's a woman?"

"They're all a bit sharp, to be honest, but yes, in one or two he addresses the recipient as 'babe.' If I get anything more, I'll ring you."

Time to return to the station and catch up with what had been happening. Rocco had organised the team that had found the phone, and Alice had been at Greco's side most of the day. Both had done well. When all this was over, he'd have to buy them a drink.

CHAPTER 46

As Calladine parked his car at the station, a woman called out to him. It was Emma Holden.

"I'm leaving tomorrow, going back to Stafford. I just wanted to say goodbye and no hard feelings," Emma said.

"Stafford? I didn't realise you lived that far away. I was hoping you'd want to hang around a little longer," Calladine said.

"I can't — there's work, and I do have a life, you know."

"You still blame me for Lydia. I understand that, there's many a dark night when I blame me too. But I'd like to see you again. Will you be coming back to Leesdon?" he asked.

"I shouldn't think so. Kieron's dead and he was the only one of my old cases I stayed in touch with when I moved away. I don't think you and me seeing each other is a good idea. Lydia is a hard act to follow, and I'm not her." She smiled. "But I didn't want to just disappear and say nothing."

"Fancy a drink? A quick one in the Wheatsheaf before you leave?"

"I haven't got time, Tom. My train leaves soon, and I want to get back home today." She kissed his cheek. "Lydia did love you, she told me so. But she was also fickle. She fell out of love as quickly as she fell in. Silly girl. I used to give her a hard time because of it."

"Lydia could've had anyone," Calladine said, "but for a short time, she chose me. I should be grateful."

"Don't be so hard on yourself. I must go. Take care, Tom Calladine. Don't get into too much trouble."

Calladine watched her walk off. Emma Holden reminded him of a time gone by, a time when he'd had Lydia in his life. He missed that. He missed having someone he could love.

As he went into the building, he met Ruth coming out.

"What kept you? I hung around in case you wanted to talk, but I've got to get home now. Anna has had Harry all day and she'll need a break," Ruth said.

"See you tomorrow, then. Is Rob coming round tonight?" Calladine asked.

"I don't think he can. Him and Julian are busy, remember, analysing all that evidence you keep throwing their way."

"Rocco and Alice? Are they still in the office?"

"No, but Greco is still working. Why not have a word? Thank him for finding your family."

* * *

"He's a bright lad, that nephew of yours," Greco said. "Tackled his assailant as a distraction so he could hide that smartwatch of his."

"Just as well it had GPS, otherwise we might never have found them."

"You and the team have done well. We've now got a solid case against Clifford Machin," Greco said.

"There are still a couple of outstanding issues," Calladine said. "He must have had help. I know there's Nathan, the lad who worked with him in the café, but he'd need muscle to carry out some of the things he did. Tackling Mark is a case in point. Someone from Machin's past, perhaps? Whoever it was, they must have made contact by phone or in person. We have Machin's phone data. I'll get onto it tomorrow."

"You don't look particularly happy, Tom. I thought you would have been more pleased, but the outcome appears to trouble you," Greco said.

Calladine sat down opposite Greco. The man had asked, so he'd tell him. "You want the truth?"

"Whatever reservations you've got, spit them out."

"I don't think Machin did this." Blunt, and the words brought a frown to Greco's face. "I don't think he's got it in him any more. There was a time when that man was capable of the most horrific crimes. He worked with a couple of real thugs — Reggie York and my cousin, Ray Fallon — and that takes a strong stomach, believe me. But that was the old Machin. This recent version is an ex-con who just wants a quiet life."

"There is forensic evidence and that doesn't lie. How d'you explain that?" Greco asked.

"I can't, not yet. But Machin is lying in hospital unable to speak up for himself. He has suffered with chronic heart failure for years, and he just isn't up to what we're accusing him of."

"Nonetheless, Tom, even you have to admit the evidence is compelling. And despite your feelings, we will compile a file for the CPS. Machin is guilty, you have to accept that. He has been in prison all these years just waiting for the opportunity to get even with you. Targeting your family was most likely always part of his plan. He wanted to hurt you, make you pay for what you did."

What Greco said sounded right, but Calladine still wasn't convinced. His instincts were twitching, and he couldn't stop the doubts from crowding his mind.

"Go home, sleep on it. We'll look at the evidence again tomorrow and try to figure out who helped Machin kidnap your mother and nephew."

Calladine left Greco's office in thoughtful mood. With so much evidence against Machin, he had no choice but to accept what was in front of his eyes. But still the doubts persisted.

He was passing the main office on his way out when a uniformed officer stopped him.

"We've had a call from Huddersfield General, sir. Clifford Machin died an hour ago. He never recovered consciousness."

Calladine knew what that meant. No trial, and given what they had on the man, the CPS would happily accept Greco's assertion that Machin was guilty. Calladine needed a drink.

CHAPTER 47

As Calladine entered his house, he tripped over a suitcase lying in the hallway. "Amy!" he called. "What's going on? What's this doing here? I nearly broke my neck!"

Amy Dean came to meet him wearing a scowl. "I'm leaving, Tom. This just isn't working. You're not interested in me, you're never home."

Calladine was confused. There wasn't supposed to be anything between the two of them anyway. That wasn't the deal. Amy was here because of the baby and to visit Julian. She was staying at his because there was more room. "Where are you going? Back to Cornwall?"

"No, Julian will put me up."

"His place has only the one bedroom. How will you manage?"

"That's my business." Amy stood looking at him, her hands on her hips. "I did think we might give things another go, and I would have liked that. You and me were good together, but I see now that I was wrong. You have no interest in rekindling what we had. You think of nothing but your work. You're a bore, Tom Calladine, and I'm sick of it."

Calladine was taken aback. This was the last thing he'd expected. "I'm sorry you think like that. But you don't have to leave. Accept things as they are, and we'll just be friends."

"I don't want to be your friend. I need more, and I thought at your time of life, you felt the same."

His time of life. Calladine's eyes widened. Were things that bad? "Long day," he muttered. "In fact, bloody long week. Why don't we go out, get a drink and talk it through?"

"My mind is made up. I'm off to Julian's. You've had all the chances you're getting."

Another one who felt like Layla, the last woman in his life. He'd miss Amy. She was good company when she wasn't prattling on about weird stuff. She marched out, slamming the front door behind her. It was back to the status quo, just him and Sam. He patted the dog. The poor beast was very understanding. Calladine had had so many different women staying here in recent times, and Sam had simply accepted them all.

But the sad fact was, he couldn't carry on like this. From now on, if he wanted someone in his life, it had to be permanent. No more flitting from woman to woman. With the next one, it was all or nothing.

He was just about to get stuck into the whisky when he heard a knock on his front door. For a moment he thought that Amy had changed her mind, but no such luck. There on his doorstep was a huge brute of a man.

He pushed his way in past Calladine and closed the door. "We need to talk," he said.

At first, Calladine had no idea who he was. He looked to be in his sixties, with sparse grey hair. "Do I know you?"

The man's eyes narrowed, as if he were trying to decide whether Calladine was serious or not. "Look closer. It's been a while."

"Sorry, but I still can't place you."

"Time changes us all, you included," the man said, "but I reckon the passing years have done you less favours than me."

"Thanks a lot. Just what I'm short of right now, a confidence boost!" But there was something familiar about him. Calladine had a bad feeling. Suddenly, he twigged. "Reggie York! I thought you were still inside."

"Spot on, you got there in the end. But I got out several years ago. Me, Ray and good ol' Cliff — the jolly threesome, we called ourselves. We did a lot of work together back in the day."

'Work' wasn't what Calladine would have called it. The three had been hardcore criminals who didn't care who they hurt or what destruction they left behind them.

"I'm the only one left now, so it's fallen to me to put the record straight." They were standing in the hallway. "Am I coming in, or do we do this standing by the front door?"

Calladine stood aside and followed the man through to the sitting room.

"You do know that Cliff had nothing to do with this case you're investigating? He was set up good and proper. And whoever is responsible did a bloody good job."

Calladine said nothing. He was curious. What did this man know, and where had that information come from?

"Cliff wanted to go straight when he got out. Of that much, I'm certain. We'd kept in touch over the years and he went on about it all the time. He wanted a new start, a new life away from Leesworth. In the early days, after he was sentenced, he was bitter. He hated you, even tried to get you bumped off a couple of times." He saw the puzzlement on Calladine's face. "You knew nothing about that? Just goes to show — hire idiots and you get crap results. But over time, he mellowed, decided it wasn't worth the aggro. So, if you're thinking this was about wanting to get even, take some sort of revenge, then you're wrong."

Reggie York fell silent. His gaze roamed around the room until it fell on the whisky bottle on the sideboard. "Ray's favourite."

"Yes, I know. Cliff told me the other night."

"You've spoken, then. Good. He'll have told you a few things about Jimmy Merrill, too, most likely."

"Yes, he did. But everything he said just reinforced his guilt. He knew things, allowed his premises to be used for drug distribution, and we have forensic evidence on a body."

York's eyes narrowed. "You do understand what 'set up' means, Calladine? I'm talking about someone clever who had the opportunity. Someone no one is looking at."

"That internet café of his was involved in drug distribution and organising two murders. I don't think the two are connected, but I can't be sure."

"They're not. The drugs are down to a Bulgarian. He runs an operation all over the North of England. Same format, relatively small amounts leaving premises for distribution on sink estates. His profits are huge — volume of outlets, you see."

"Did Cliff know this?" Calladine asked.

"Cliff was a victim every bit as much as all the others who were roped in. He told me he was being leaned on. This Bulgarian had plenty of muscle to call on. In the end, Cliff had no choice. But it did bring in a bob or two — useful, as that café of his didn't make much."

"And you believed him?" Calladine asked.

"Cliff wouldn't lie to me. He never has, and he wouldn't start now. Fallon was a different matter. Fallon would lie through his eyeteeth to get his own ends. Cliff was scared. I'm surprised he didn't tell you."

The notion of Clifford Machin being scared almost made Calladine laugh. But he was thinking of a very different Machin from the one who'd recently left prison. "I think he tried," he nodded at the whisky, "the night we drank most of that."

Reggie York stood up and went to the sideboard, took the bottle, two glasses and poured a measure in each. "As for the killings, that's a different matter. Those are down to some weirdo who calls himself 'Snowdrop.' Amused Cliff at first, that name. But it turned out to be no laughing matter. Snowdrop's another bastard who threatened him. Said he'd torch the place with Cliff in it if he didn't play ball."

"Do you have any idea who this Snowdrop is, or where he's from?"

"No idea. He could be another Bulgarian, I suppose, or Polish or summat similar. The young lass who made the drops was, for sure." He handed Calladine a glass.

"My family was targeted," Calladine said. "They're lucky to be alive. Cliff hated me, you said so yourself, so that would be a perfect way of getting back at me."

Reggie York downed his whisky in one. He laughed. "Cliff wouldn't waste his time, Calladine. If he'd really wanted to make you suffer, he'd have dumped you somewhere well out of the way and put bullets in both your legs. You'd have suffered a long, drawn-out death with little chance of being found."

Calladine shuddered. He was probably right. And now he remembered Cliff's confusion when he'd mentioned his mother. Cliff hadn't known about the Buckleys.

"I do have my doubts about Cliff's guilt," Calladine admitted. "I haven't worked out the details yet, but I will."

"This is close to home. Look for someone who knows the Merrill case, or has access to it and can fiddle the forensics."

That was serious stuff. Calladine felt sick to his stomach.

Reggie York slammed the glass down on the table and made for the front door. "Put it right, and that's a warning. I'm not asking you. I don't want Cliff taking the blame for the drugs or the murders. When this is done, we'll speak again."

"Before you go, do you have a name for this Bulgarian?"

"No, but I'll get it and be in touch."

CHAPTER 48

Day 8

The following day the team were in good form. It was obvious from the banter that they believed Machin was guilty and they had found their man. What they needed to do now was find the young woman who'd made the drugs drop at the café — Alina — presumably the one Reggie York had spoken about.

"Machin's mobile data, did it reveal anything?" Calladine asked.

"No, but it is a contract phone. If he did have a burner, we haven't found it," Rocco said. "Do we keep looking?"

Calladine shook his head.

"Nathan is being brought in," Ruth said. "I sent a couple of uniforms to get him, just in case he decided to do a runner."

"Let him try," Calladine growled. Another sleepless night hadn't sweetened his mood. First Amy leaving like that, followed by Reggie York making his unannounced visit. He'd said a lot, but what did it actually add up to? Thinking about the conversation later, Calladine had to admit that the theory was sound. The drug dealing, he could understand. It was a way for Machin to make extra money with little effort. But who would want to set up Clifford Machin for murder, and why?

But perhaps that wasn't what this was about — not Machin, and not getting back at him for some long-forgotten misdemeanour. Perhaps it was all about the money, the ransomware demand, pure and simple.

The killer could have pulled it off. The Buckleys might have rolled over and paid up, or even negotiated. In which case, the killer would have been a wealthy man. If he got wind that someone else was in the frame, would he try again? Buckley Pharmaceuticals still didn't have their systems back up and running, and Roxy Atkins thought that it was highly unlikely they would without the decryption key.

It was a sobering thought, but whoever was behind this had nothing to lose.

"Greco is pleased with the outcome," Ruth said, smiling. "He told me earlier that the team did well, you in particular."

Calladine shook his head. "It's not over yet."

"Greco thinks it is. We'll track the drugs back as far as possible, but whether we're successful or not, we got Moira Haigh and Kieron Ramsey's killer, and that's what matters."

Calladine felt weird. How come he was the only one who could see the cracks? He retreated into his office and rang Simon Buckley. He wanted to warn him, disguising the call's importance as simply asking about Eve.

"She's home and doing fine for now, so's Mark," Simon told him. "Mum had a narrow escape. I expect the full extent of what could have happened will hit her later."

"Does she remember anything about the incident?"

"She was drugged and out of it for a long time, Tom. Consequently, she doesn't recall a thing. Mark, though, says their assailant was big, strong and he wore a mask over his face."

"Keep an eye on her. I'm serious, Simon. She's still delicate. Don't let her leave the house on her own."

"Eve's tough. She has a mind of her own. Don't underestimate her, Tom."

Simon wasn't listening. Despite not wanting to, Calladine would have to get heavy. "Please, Simon, watch over your family carefully. I'm not sure this is over yet."

"You're worrying me now, Tom. You know something. What aren't you telling me? You say you don't think this is over yet, but how can that be? I'd heard that the man who did it is dead."

"There are still questions I haven't got answers to," Calladine said. "The truth is, Simon, I'm not sure who is guilty and who isn't. Just do as I ask and keep a close eye on your family. Don't let them leave the house alone. Have a word with your sister Samantha too, and her family."

"Okay, I'll do that."

Calladine's mobile rang, showing an unknown number.

"Calladine, it's Reggie. I've got a name for you, the drug dealer we spoke about. Go get the bastard, and beat the truth out of him if you have to."

"That's not how it works, Reggie. Do you have any proof that this 'name' is the dealer?"

"Do your job, man! You're the bloody copper, not me. This name has cost me. I've worked most of the night, spoken to people I'd rather forget I knew, called in favours and parted with cold, hard cash. My job is done. Now it's your turn."

"This name — he's the individual who supplied the drugs to Cliff?"

"Yes, so don't slip up. Arrest the bugger and question him. I don't expect to hear that he's back on the streets any time soon."

All very well, but without solid evidence, locking him up was impossible. "I'll do my best, Reggie. That's all I can promise."

"I'll give you one day, Calladine. If you haven't found the bastard by then, I'll have him sorted myself."

"I don't advise it, Reggie. You could end up back inside."

"In that case, get on with it. Now listen. His name is Andrei Lazarov. He's a Bulgarian."

Reggie York ended the call. Calladine sat and thought for a while. How much should he trust him? But he couldn't see what Reggie had to gain by lying. He simply wanted justice for Cliff.

Calladine entered the name into the database. Lazarov had a record and had spent time inside for dealing. But there was nothing recent. The address given for him was in a run-down part of Huddersfield.

Rocco interrupted him. "Nathan is in the soft interview room. He's giving a description of that girl to Ruth and the forensic artist from the Duggan. Nathan hasn't said much yet, and the sketch is way off being complete, but something struck me."

"What was that?"

"That young, foreign girl we spoke to at the Ash house. From the way Nathan is describing her, she sounds like a real possibility," Rocco said.

CHAPTER 49

Gina Haigh was relieved at her and Arron Cookson's release, while Noah Ash remained in custody. The Family Liaison Officer told Gina that the man who'd killed her aunt had been caught.

Gina had searched her aunt's house from top to bottom, looking for her will. Moira was bound to have had one — she was that kind of woman.

"You could have it all wrong, G. What's to say she left the place to you?" Arron asked.

"Because I'm all the family she had, and even she wouldn't be so mean."

He shrugged. "She didn't like you much."

Gina had emptied all the drawers and rifled through the cupboards. She'd made a hell of a mess, but still there was no will. "Where would she put the bloody thing! I hate this place. Once I know for sure it's mine, it's being sold and we'll move on."

That got Cookson's interest. "How much will it fetch, do you reckon?"

"A lot. It's detached and Leesworth is sought after, apparently. I took a wander past the estate agent's yesterday afternoon. This place could be worth a packet."

"There'll be a solicitor involved. People usually go to them when they want a will doing. Perhaps he's got it."

Gina groaned and pulled a face. "This is a small place and there's only the one. The office is on the High Street."

"What's wrong with that?"

"The solicitor is called Zoe Calladine. It's an unusual name. She's bound to be related to that detective we spoke to."

"So what? You've every right to know what's in Moira's will."

There was a knock on the front door. Gina and Cooksie looked at each other.

"Who the 'ell's that?" he asked. "You expecting someone, G?"

Gina peeped through the blinds at the front window. "It's some girl. I think it's the one that knew Noah."

"I'll sort it."

Arron Cookson went to the front door and found an anxious-looking Alina waiting on the step.

"You have to go," he said. "You can't come here. Noah's been locked up. He can't harm you."

"I'm not afraid of Noah, idiot!" she said. "Who do you think supplied me? It's him I'm afraid of, and you should be too."

"Why, what's his beef with me and Gina? I never met the man."

"This part of his operation is over. He's not going to allow anyone who was connected with it to live. You have to help me. I need a place to hide. You have a place some distance from here, you went there with your girl."

"The caravan? You can't go there, the police know about it."

"I'm desperate. If he finds me, I'm dead," Alina said.

Arron Cookson shrugged. "Sorry, love, but you'll have to take your chances. I don't know this man you're on about and I can't help you."

The truth was, Cooksie had never thought about the chain of supply. Ash turned up on the Hobfield, doled out the packets, collected the money and that was that. Cooksie had only been on the periphery of the operation. As far as he was concerned, Noah Ash was in charge.

"Noah supplied you with drugs of all types. You made good money. He in turn had a supplier, and I acted as a go-between. Noah is locked up, and another of the people involved is dead. If he gets rid of me, there is only you left to speak up against him."

Cooksie's eyes widened. "What? You're talking about some big bad drugs boss? I don't even know a name. I can't help the police."

"Andrei doesn't know that. When he cleans up, he likes to be thorough. He will not want the likes of me, or you, telling the police what we know."

"Andrei who? On second thoughts, don't tell me. The less I know, the better."

"Too late, you are involved. His name is Andrei Lazarov, he is Bulgarian like me."

"Did he kill Gina's aunt?"

"No, why would he?"

Gina had been listening from the hallway. "Send her packing. We can't help her."

"You could hide me for a few days. That's all I'd need," Alina said.

Gina Haigh came forward and stood facing the girl, staring hard at her. "Not a good idea. We do that and this drugs baron of yours will come after us. Why would we want that? Get lost, and don't come back."

"Don't say you weren't warned. If he finds you, Andrei will want answers. He will want to know what happened to the man in the café, and why the police are all over that place. He'll think Ash told them things, and he will find you too."

Cooksie tried to weigh up his chances. Was she right? Did this Lazarov know about him? "I think G's right, you should do one before he finds you."

"Okay, but know this. Andrei is a violent man, he will not hesitate to destroy you both."

Cooksie watched her turn and walk off down the road. He had no idea how she'd found them, but the fact that she had wasn't good. He went back into the house.

"She might have a point, G. This Bulgarian bloke could come after us. He could know that we're involved."

"That means we're dead!" she screamed. "You sold that stuff. You got the drugs off Ash. This man could know your face, your name, everything."

"Even if he does, why would he want to kill me?"

"Because, like she said, he's clearing up! Getting rid of people who can testify against him."

"What d'you want to do?"

"I'm going to see that solicitor, see if she's got Moira's will. You stay here and lay low."

* * *

Gina Haigh hurried down the road towards the nearest bus stop. Suddenly she was terrified. This Andrei sounded like a bad man, violent. She dare not risk him finding her or Cooksie.

The bus would be along shortly. A quick visit to the solicitors and then she and Cooksie would get a bed and breakfast in the city. A few days lying low, put the house on the market and then move to another area for a fresh start.

But she'd run out of luck.

"Not so fast," a foreign voice said.

A black saloon pulled up beside her and a strong pair of hands pulled her inside. She didn't know the man. Gina's heart missed a beat.

"Where did Alina go?"

"I've no idea. I don't know any Alina."

"You're lying. She was at your house. Did you help her, give her money? Perhaps you rang the police?"

"I didn't, I wouldn't. Let me out."

"I can't trust you. You are involved, you and your boyfriend. You know people, Alina for a start. The police will question you again and you will tell them about me."

"I won't, Andrei! I promise. I won't tell them anything."

He hammered his palms on the steering wheel. "See? You know my name!"

"That was Alina, she told us."

He started the car and drove fast out of Lowermill, up into the hills.

"Let me go!"

"Can't do that." Minutes later, he pulled into a layby where another, much older car was waiting for them. "Get out," Andrei Lazarov ordered.

The man in the second car shoved her into the driver's seat and locked the door from outside.

Gina was frantic, she'd no idea what was happening. She hammered on the window with both fists. "Let me go!" she screamed. "Please, Andrei, don't do this."

The last thing Gina Haigh saw was the muzzle of a gun pointing in through the driver's side window. One shot, and she knew no more.

"Torch the lot," Lazarov told the man. "And make it quick. I've got things to do."

CHAPTER 50

Noah Ash's mother eyed Calladine and Ruth with suspicion. "You've arrested my Noah, what d'you want now?"

"The young woman who visits occasionally — Alina. Have you seen her?" Calladine asked.

The woman shook her head. "She must have gone home. Noah is in custody, so there's no need for her to hang around."

"Do you know where she lives?"

"I know very little about her."

"Did Alina ever talk about any friends or relatives she could have gone to?" he asked.

"Alina didn't mix much — well, not that she told me about. She did have friends in Huddersfield. Noah often visited her there."

"Okay, but if she turns up, ring us at once."

They made their way back to the car, Calladine thoughtful. "Alina was supplied by one Alexei Lazarov, he lives in Huddersfield, so that makes sense."

"Where did that name come from? It's a new one on me," Ruth said.

"I've been given some information — his name, among other things," Calladine said.

She shrugged. "Okay, an informant, then. So, what's Lazarov's connection with Machin?"

"Does there have to be one? Noah Ash acted as pick-up boy, and Alina collected the drugs for him. There was no need for Lazarov to get involved with Machin or Ash."

"Is Lazarov a major player in the drugs world?" Ruth asked.

"It was a big enough operation," he said.

"Until now. But his little empire has collapsed around him, so Alina could be in danger," Ruth said.

"Which is why we need to find her."

"Does this mean the two aspects of this case are not down to Machin alone? Is he the killer and involved with the drugs, or just the killer?"

"Neither," Calladine said. "Machin allowed his premises to be used by the drug gang for pick-ups. No doubt he was well paid for it. But that's as far as it went."

"You worry me at times, Calladine. You sound so sure. But we have evidence, solid forensics. How do you get round that one?"

"Like I said, I've been given some information — well, more a suggestion, really, but I think it might be valid."

"Care to share?"

"Not yet."

"Who gave you this information? Anyone I know?"

"No."

"And the murders, who do we pin those on if not him?" Ruth asked, truly puzzled now. "This Lazarov?"

"No," Calladine said. "I believe he's responsible for the drugs alone."

* * *

"The problem now is where to start looking for Alina," Calladine said. "Does Nathan know anything about this girl, other than that she's involved with the dealer?"

Ruth shook her head. "He says not. She wasn't a chatty sort, apparently. But we could ask Noah Ash. He dealt with her too and she went to his home."

"Okay. Have him brought up and we'll give it a go."

Calladine's mobile beeped. It was Julian.

"The DNA extracted from the blood on the curtain Moira Haigh's body was wrapped in is a match to that taken from your nephew's T-shirt. But it's not Machin, and there's nothing on the database that does match it."

"What about DNA taken for elimination purposes?" Calladine asked.

"Again, no match. I do know my job, Tom," Julian said, and sniffed.

"Sorry, Julian, I wasn't getting at you."

"What do you want anyway? I sense you've got some theory in your head that you're not sharing."

"Just tired, Julian. Don't read anything into it. Did Amy get to yours okay?" Quick change of subject — he didn't want Julian asking too many questions about his reasons for the tests. "She didn't have to leave like that. I was more than happy for her to stay."

"She's a complex woman, hard to understand sometimes. Amy likes you, Tom. I think she was hoping for more."

"Me and Amy were well and truly over a while ago. I thought she understood that."

"No matter, she'll probably return home soon."

Calladine hung up, then his phone rang again. It was Reggie York.

"Calladine, our drug-dealing friend has been active again. He took a girl, drove up over the tops, put her in a beat-up car, shot her and torched the lot."

"Where has this information come from, Reggie?"

"Contacts, and that's all you're getting."

"D'you know who she was?"

"No idea. Not my problem anyway. Our man is cleaning up. Soon, he'll drop off the radar. Sort him, Calladine, you're running out of time."

* * *

Calladine hurried into the incident room. "Ruth, we have to go out."

"Where to? Why all the hurry?"

"It's possible the girl we're looking for has been killed. If my info's right she's in a burnt-out car up on the tops."

"Where on the tops? There's a lot of it sitting above Leesdon in case you hadn't noticed."

"He won't have taken her far. Unlikely he had the time."

Ruth was confused. "Tom, who are we talking about? Who told you this tale?"

They made for his car. Getting in behind the wheel, Calladine gave Ruth a quick glance. She deserved something, he'd kept a lot about this case to himself and it wasn't fair. Like she'd said, she was his partner.

"Reggie York," he said. "He was a pal of—"

"Yes, I know who he is, but why is he talking to you all of a sudden?"

"Because we have something in common. Both of us believe that Clifford Machin is innocent of killing Kieron and Moira."

Ruth groaned. "Not that again! How much proof d'you need? You're doing my head in, and not just mine either. Greco's another one who doesn't understand where this idea of yours has come from."

"Stray DNA."

"I'm not with you."

"There is DNA on the curtain Moira was wrapped in and it matches that found on Mark's T-shirt," Calladine said.

Ruth shrugged. "So? The killer had help."

"There's no evidence of that."

"Alright, suppose just for one moment that I go along with your theory — who d'you reckon the killer is?"

"Someone who calls himself Snowdrop," he said.

"Tom, given what we know, I'd presumed that was Machin."

"No, and I'm sure that our killer works alone. He's after the ransomware money and chose Cliff Machin's café

209

because he made the perfect scapegoat. I bet they disposed of those bodies that way for the same reason."

"It's a bit far-fetched. What about the drug dealing? How does that fit in?" Ruth said.

"It doesn't. That is a different case entirely. I bet that if we investigated, we'd find other businesses in the area with the same set-up."

"Do you have any idea who the killer is?" Ruth asked.

"Yes." Calladine didn't elaborate. Ruth was fast losing patience.

"Want to tell me, or is this some game you're playing?"

"It's no game, Ruth, and I'm kicking myself for not realising before. It was something Reggie York said to me, and I think he was right."

Suddenly, Ruth grabbed his arm and pointed to a layby where a smouldering car was parked up. There was a fire engine in attendance, and the fire-fighters had arrived soon enough to prevent the vehicle being totally destroyed. The upper doors and roof were still intact.

"Looks like we've found it."

"There's a body too — see? In the front seat. Will you ring the Duggan, get a team out here?"

CHAPTER 51

"One thing's for certain," Natasha Barrington said. "This was no accident. She was shot in the head and locked inside. There's no key in the ignition either."

"Poor girl. No chance of escape. Who does that to someone?" Ruth asked.

Calladine was looking at the road just past the burnt car. He could see clear tyre marks where whoever had brought her had driven off again. "He took off at speed in that direction."

"Towards Huddersfield," Ruth noted. "D'you know who this is?" Gruesome as it was, she was peering at the partially burned body through the cracked sooty window. "Look, Tom. See her hair? If I'm not mistaken, the ends are a green colour."

That meant this was Gina Haigh. But what had she done to get herself killed? "In that case, it's not who I thought it was. Still, I'll run what's happened past Noah Ash, see what he has to say."

"There's a bag here with a mobile in it," Natasha called. "We might get something. The outer case is a bit deformed by the fire, but the sim could be okay."

"Name, Calladine. Tell me who did this," Ruth demanded.

"An individual called Andrei Lazarov. He's a Bulgarian and the one behind the drug dealing. He supplied to any number of premises for distribution to users by people like Noah Ash and Arron Cookson."

"And Reggie York gave you the name?" she asked. "Why would he do that? A man with his reputation is more likely to be in league with Lazarov."

"Reggie's time of working with the criminal fraternity is over. These days all he wants is a quiet life," Calladine said.

"What's Machin got to do with it?"

"Nothing, and that's the point. York gave me the information about Lazarov to help clear Cliff's name."

"But Machin was happy for his place to be used?" Ruth said.

"Yes, but he was leaned on."

Ruth was confused. This was the first time she'd heard any of this. "Is the case ours, or do we pass it over to Huddersfield? This does lead back to that internet café."

"I'll speak to Greco and see how he wants to play it. The girl was killed on our patch, and Lazarov's drugs were being peddled on the Hobfield, so we do have an interest."

There was nothing more to do here. Gina's body, if that's who it was, would be taken to the Duggan for the PM.

* * *

"Noah, a young woman you know has met a rather grisly end. She's been murdered by a Bulgarian drug dealer called Lazarov. It wasn't pleasant — she was almost burnt to a crisp."

Noah's eyes widened. "You're trying to frighten me. That can't be right. You mustn't say things like that."

"Gina Haigh. You did know her, didn't you? She was Cooksie's girlfriend."

"Are you saying that Gina is really dead?"

Calladine nodded. "That young woman, Alina, who I met at your house the other day, where is she?"

"How should I know?" Noah said.

"We've got Nathan from the internet café helping with an identikit of the girl who dropped off the drugs. My colleague here reckons she's very like the girl we saw at your house. Anything to say to that?"

"You won't be able to stop him. No one can. Lazarov does whatever he wants and trusts no one, particularly those who work for him. The girl you saw with my mum is the one who does the drop-off — Alina. She was hanging around my house because she is supposed to keep an eye on me, make sure I toe the line and don't attract your attention."

"She'll be disappointed then. You're currently in very big trouble, Noah. How much does she know?"

"A lot more than me. She's been working with Lazarov for a long time."

Calladine leaned towards Ruth, who was sitting beside him. "Circulate a description and get the identikit to the press the moment it's ready. I want her bringing in."

"Can I have a word outside?" she said.

Calladine followed her out. Ruth didn't look happy.

"This dealer is dangerous. We bring in his people and you will have to watch your step."

"I'll take the risk. He needs catching and Alina can tell me where he hangs out."

Ruth looked doubtful. "If she tells you anything at all."

"I'll take that chance."

Ruth marched off towards the office. "I need a coffee."

Calladine followed her, that wasn't a bad idea. Coffee would wake him up, sharpen his brain and help him weigh up the risks. Bring her in, or pass the whole lot over to Huddersfield?

"Hi, you two." Rob was standing by the kettle. "Sorry, one of the uniforms let me in and I helped myself to a drink while I was waiting."

"You're more than welcome." Ruth smiled at him.

"That girl — we got into her mobile, it is Gina Haigh. I told Alice and she's arranging to tell Arron Cookson."

"Thanks, Rob, I did think as much," Calladine said.

"You're busy, interviewing someone, I hear." Rob looked at Ruth. "Still on for tomorrow?"

"Yes. My place, no later than ten, and bring food," she said.

"My pleasure," Rob said.

Calladine watched him leave the office and close the door behind him. "You've got him well trained."

"You have to start as you mean to go on. I'll go back in — don't be long."

Calladine was alone in the main office. His eyes wandered to the mug Rob Harris had just put on the tray. It hadn't been washed and would still have his saliva on it. Without a second thought, he put it in an evidence bag and hid it in his briefcase.

CHAPTER 52

Alina Slovenski had been apprehended just as she was about to board a train for London and brought to the station kicking and screaming. She'd changed from the quiet, unassuming girl they'd met at the Ash house to a wild banshee, spitting obscenities at the officers who were trying to process her.

"You will die for this!" she screamed. "Andrei will not allow you to live!"

"Andrei isn't here, and anyway he's not above the law, young lady," Calladine said. "You need to calm down. We'll get you a solicitor, but we only want to ask you a few questions."

"No! I will not tell you anything!"

Alina launched herself at a uniformed constable, hitting him in the eye and sending him crashing to the floor.

"That's it!" Calladine shouted. "You've had your chance. Now I have no choice but to arrest you for assaulting an officer. Take her away," he told the four additional uniforms who'd been called in.

"Feisty little madam, isn't she?" Rocco said. "What's she done?"

"Yeah, that's some temper she's got. I want to talk to her about the dealing at the café," Calladine said.

"Tom, can I have a word?"

It was Greco. Calladine followed him to his office.

"Well done with the drug-dealing aspect of the case. Not connected to the murders then?" Greco asked.

Calladine shook his head. "No, completely separate."

"Not entirely. The link was Machin."

Calladine didn't comment.

"A team from West Yorkshire police have been investigating Lazarov for some time. They want to take control now. The operation he leads is huge and it extends well beyond Machin's internet café."

"But the final outlet for some of the drugs he peddles is around here," Calladine said. "He used local people — Ash and Cookson, for starters. And Alina? What do we do with her? She's just given one of our officers a black eye, and I want to charge her. And that poor girl Gina Haigh was murdered on our patch, too. That layby—"

"The layby where Gina was killed is bang on the West Yorkshire border, Tom. As for Alina, officers from Huddersfield are coming over to collect her. She has valuable information about Lazarov that will help them. The Duggan will hand over the PM report on Gina and all forensics too. Don't push me on this, Tom. You've worked hard enough. You've sorted the dealing, got the name of a major player, and the killer of Ramsey and Haigh. A good call all round. And that's not all," Greco continued. "The Cheshire force found the body of Jimmy Merrill where you said it would be, in Lowmere. More evidence of Machin's guilt, I think."

"How did they know it was him? I shouldn't think there'd be much left after all this time," said Calladine.

"He wore a crucifix on a chain around his neck. It had his name engraved on the back."

So, Machin had been right. "Will his remains be analysed for DNA, to confirm how he died and give a clue as to the identity of his killer?"

"Yes, but we already know who killed him, don't we? How else could Machin know where Merrill was?" Greco said.

"Is that it?"

Greco nodded. "I must say, Tom, for someone who has just cracked a complex case, you don't look very happy."

"Just tired, Stephen. A good night's sleep and I'll be fine."

Calladine returned to the office to find Ruth packing up for the day. "I'm off tomorrow. Me and Rob are taking Harry on a picnic. So, no phone calls — and don't go finding any more bodies."

He smiled. "I'll do my best."

Calladine collected his stuff and made for his car. He was off to see Julian, but he'd have to tread carefully, if he was right, the next bit would upset people he was fond of.

* * *

"What's this?" Julian asked.

"Come on, Julian, what does it look like?" Calladine replied.

"A mug?"

"Exactly," Calladine said, "and I'd like you to run a DNA test on it. When you've got a result, would you check it against that of the unknown DNA you're sitting on?"

"As you wish. Am I allowed to know who drank out of this mug last?"

"No, that would spoil the surprise. I would appreciate you rushing this through, Julian. The safety of people we know could depend on it."

"This cryptic stance doesn't suit you, Tom. Normally I wouldn't agree to such cloak-and-dagger tactics, but I know you and appreciate that you will have your reasons."

"Too bloody true I do."

CHAPTER 53

Day 9

Ruth had taken the day off, Rocco was in Greco's office having a chat, so that left Calladine and Alice to sort out the statements and files relating to both cases.

"It's a shame about Gina. She didn't deserve to die that way," Alice said.

"No, she didn't, Alice. Let's hope that Lazarov gets what's coming to him, and the West Yorkshire police don't bugger it up," Calladine said.

"They have to find him first," Alice said. "Andrei Lazarov lives with his mother in a place called Lockwood on the outskirts of Huddersfield. He hasn't been back in two days and she says she's no idea where he is."

"The property will be watched."

"He is one dangerous man. Kills without a second thought. What makes people like that?"

"I don't know, Alice, but he's not our problem any more. Let's get this lot sorted and then we can take the rest of the day off too."

Rocco returned to the main office, looking very pleased with himself. Calladine eyed him sceptically. What nonsense had Greco filled his head with?

"How's your mum?" Rocco asked.

"Recovering well. She's very resilient, is Eve," Calladine said.

Alice was looking at her phone. "Aww, isn't that sweet. Ruth, Rob and little Harry. He's fishing, got his bright blue wellies on too, bless him."

Calladine took a look and immediately felt uneasy. They were at the river near the reservoir up in the hills. Granted it was a lovely day and that was a great spot, but it was lonely, and he worried for their safety. He had to have those results off Julian. This needed bringing to an end.

He picked up his mobile and rang him. "Any joy with the mug?" he asked.

"I admit to being confused, Tom. There is a match. The blood on the curtain, that on Mark's T-shirt and the saliva on that mug all came from the same individual."

Calladine's heart began to pound. Julian's confirmation made his theory real, and the implications were horrendous.

"Who are we looking at?" Julian asked.

"Rob Harris."

Calladine didn't wait for the inevitable questions. He finished the call and went to find Greco. The man wasn't going to like this but that couldn't be helped. Ruth and little Harry could be in danger.

Greco was putting the phone down as Calladine knocked on his office door.

"Professor Batho has just told me."

Good old Julian. He'd realised that this sort of news was better coming from him, the expert.

"Sorry, Stephen, it rubbishes everyone's assumptions about Machin and gives us a problem."

"How long have you known?" Greco asked.

"My instincts have been twitching from the start," Calladine said, "but what clinched it was a comment someone made recently. A friend of Machin's told me that he'd been set up, and that whoever was responsible had to be able to fiddle the forensics. Normally I'd disregard something like that, but the words stuck, and the more I thought about it, the more it made sense. I trust Julian absolutely, and that only left Harris."

"Good call. I took little notice of your doubts, and I apologise. You trust your instincts, something I have always had a problem with," Greco said.

"Harris is a dangerous man, Stephen," Calladine said. "Right now, he is with Ruth and her son, fishing in the river up from the res. Ruth has no idea about him. I haven't discussed any of this with her."

"We'll get up there, bring Harris in. Are you able to ring Ruth, get her to make an excuse and go home?"

"The signal is bad," Calladine said. "We have no choice but to go up there ourselves."

CHAPTER 54

"When we get good weather, this is an idyllic spot." Ruth smiled. "I've been coming up here since I was a kid. Calladine even remembers when the res up there was built."

"It is lovely countryside, you're very lucky," Rob said.

Ruth proffered a plastic box. "Another sandwich? Please eat them, I'm not taking any of this home."

"Is the boy alright? He's very quiet."

"He's having his usual nap. He's over there under the parasol. He's fine."

"Want to go for a walk?"

Ruth was surprised Rob had even asked the question. "We can't leave him. He might wake up."

"Like you said, he's asleep, he's quite safe."

"If we go anywhere, we'll wait until Harry wakes up. Sorry, Rob, that's how it is with kids. They are a huge responsibility." This wasn't what she expected of him. It was weird. Perhaps Tom had a point. What did she really know about this man?

Rob pointed to the road. "There's a car coming."

Ruth squinted into the sun. It was Greco's car, but she didn't tell Rob that.

"They're turning into the car park. So much for our peace and quiet. Hope it's not hordes of shrieking kids," Rob said. "Want to move on? We could take the path further up the hill to the lake."

Ruth shook her head. That was not a good idea. "No, I don't. A body was fished out of there just the other day. It'll be a long time before I can sit on the banks of Doveclough Lake again."

He smiled. "You're far too sensitive."

She saw Tom walking towards them and groaned. "I told you," she shouted to him. "This is my day off. Take the work stuff and go back to the station."

Calladine nodded at Harris and sat down on the blanket beside Ruth. "There's not much going on, so I thought I'd take a wander up, see if you'd made anything nice to eat."

"Help yourself, there's a ton of sandwiches," she said.

"Where's Harry?"

"Over there under the parasol in the shade of that tree, fast asleep. Why?"

"Mind if I take a peek? I've not seen him in a while."

This wasn't the usual Calladine. What was he up to? "Promise not to wake him." Ruth got to her feet and the two of them walked across to her son.

"I want you to take him, go to the car and drive down to the first layby. There are officers waiting there."

"What's going on, Tom? What's this about?"

"Don't argue with me, Ruth. Just do as I ask."

His face said it all. Ruth had known him long enough to realise that this was no joke. Something was very wrong but she'd no idea what. Without further argument, she took Harry and got in the car.

* * *

"Where's she gone?" Rob Harris joined him.

"Somewhere safe, away from you," Calladine said.

Calladine watched his face, saw the confusion there, followed by anger. "What is this? Jealousy? Wish you'd thought of bringing Ruth up here yourself? Hard luck. I got her first."

"Nothing like that, Harris. I got Ruth and Harry out of the way because you're a dangerous man — the man I've been chasing since Kieron Ramsey was murdered. It was you who killed him, and Moira Haigh. You targeted her and the Buckleys with ransomware, and kidnapped Eve and Mark Buckley when they didn't pay up. You are Snowdrop."

Rob Harris laughed out loud. "Very clever. Your theory might be correct, Calladine, but you have no proof. Without that, Machin is guilty and I remain a free man."

Calladine shrugged. "You're wrong, Harris. You made mistakes."

Harris moved closer to Calladine. "I do not make mistakes. I plan. I am meticulous in what I do."

"You're human and you slipped up twice. Both times I collected the evidence and now you, Dr Harris, are going to pay the price."

Harris spun round, ready to make a run for it, but there were uniforms coming up the path and on the brow of the hill. He was surrounded.

EPILOGUE

"I hope you're satisfied, Calladine. You put paid to that budding relationship good and proper," Ruth said.

"He was a bloody psychopath, Ruth! What's wrong with you? I thought you'd have spotted it early on," Calladine said.

"I thought he was nice."

"What's 'nice' when it's at home? Harris conned you. He conned everyone. Anyway, you should be relieved. You're safe and came to no harm."

"I went out with him, invited him to my home. He played with Harry, for goodness' sake."

"Just don't make the same mistake again. In future, I'll vet your dates first, then you'll know you're safe."

Ruth rolled her eyes. "Given we've just wrapped that one up, what does Greco want you for so early in the morning?"

"He didn't say."

"How are you finding him?" she asked.

"Tolerable. You?"

"The same. Once you get to know him, he's actually okay. I'll make some coffee while you have your chat. But I want chapter and verse when you're done — no fobbing me off."

Calladine made his way to Greco's office and found him behind his desk, hard at it.

Greco looked up. "Well done again on the Harris case. But it's the dealing aspect I wanted to talk about now. West Yorkshire have lost Lazarov. He left Leesworth and hasn't been seen since. However, he has left a somewhat grisly reminder of his presence among us."

"More bodies?"

Greco didn't answer. "You were given information about him by one Reggie York, I believe?"

Calladine nodded. "Reggie gave me Lazarov's name."

"And we passed it on to West Yorkshire. Lazarov used a number of aliases but that is his real name."

"So, why does this matter to us?" Calladine asked.

"We believe Lazarov has killed York."

"His body's been found?"

"Not exactly. Parts of it. So far, an arm and a torso, in different locations. DNA confirmed it was him."

"Poor Reggie. He didn't deserve that."

"West Yorkshire say that Lazarov is getting even and that we need to be on our guard. You busted his operation at Machin's café and arrested his operatives. He's a vengeful man with a reputation to maintain. Bagging himself a seasoned detective who'd given him the run-around would do him no harm."

"West Yorkshire should have been quicker off the mark, caught him while they had the chance. Now Lazarov is a threat for the future that we could all do without," Calladine said. He felt suddenly ill at ease. "You think I'm in danger?"

"The chief constable is certain of it. He told me to talk to you and ask what you'd like us to do."

"Protection? Even if I agree, that can't carry on for ever."

"There's always retirement, Tom."

Calladine glared at him. As far as he was concerned, retirement was a dirty word. "I'll take my chances, if it's all the same to you. I've done battle with the best of them and I'm still in one piece. Lazarov will have gone into hiding to lick his wounds. By the time he gets his act together, he'll have forgotten all about me."

"It's your choice. I think you're making a mistake, but as you wish." Greco sighed. "I'll have a word with the chief constable later."

"What about Harris?" Calladine asked. "Do we have any idea what motivated him to kill? He's a psychopath, have the psychologists had a go at him?"

"He was reticent at first, but once he got going, there was no stopping him. He doesn't like older women much, and particularly not successful ones. His mother had him late in life and ran her own business to the detriment of looking after him. He was sent away to boarding school where he was bullied and frequently beaten up. On occasions he was hospitalised. He blamed his mother, not the bullies, and vowed to get even with her, but she died before he got the chance."

"So, he hated his mother and was frustrated because he could do nothing about it."

Greco nodded. "Looks that way. Plus, he had a thing about being in a position to outwit authority. He tampered with evidence and hindered our investigations, including his own DNA profile for elimination purposes on the database He also had access to old cases, which is how he knew all about Machin."

It made sense. Calladine was just annoyed that he'd not spotted any of this earlier.

"I've spoken to DC Rockliffe and suggested he might like to go for DS. He's a good officer and well up for the job."

Calladine agreed, somewhat surprised. Was there room at Leesdon for two DSs? He certainly didn't want to lose Ruth. "Does he like the idea?"

"I imagine so, but he wants to discuss it with you first."

"We'll have a chat. Is that all?"

"For now, but remember what I said — watch your back, Tom. Lazarov is a vengeful murderer and he's got his sights on you."

Calladine returned to the main office and helped himself to one of the coffees Ruth had made. "He didn't want much. A bit of praise. Were the team okay after all the hard work and trauma, that sort of thing." Calladine saw no point in upsetting Ruth by telling her about his possible fate.

"Rocco wants to go for sergeant, did he tell you that?" Ruth said.

Calladine nodded. "He did, but we'll have to see. That could have consequences."

"I know, and I've told him, so he's buggered off in a strop," she said.

"We'll have to let this play out. Rocco is ambitious, we can't blame him for that."

"So am I, Tom. I'd quite like to be a DI. Now, if you retired, we could all move up one."

THE END

FREE KINDLE BOOKS

DO YOU LOVE FREE AND BARGAIN BOOKS?

Do you love mysteries, historical fiction and romance? Join 1000s of readers enjoying great books through our mailing list. You'll get new releases and great deals every week from one of the UK's leading independent publishers.

Join today, and you'll get your first bargain book this month!

Follow us on Facebook, Twitter and Instagram @joffebooks

Thank you for reading this book. If you enjoyed it please leave feedback on Amazon, and if there is anything we missed or you have a question about then please get in touch. The author and publishing team appreciate your feedback and time reading this book.

We're very grateful to eagle-eyed readers who take the time to contact us. Please send any errors you find to corrections@joffebooks.com

Made in the USA
Las Vegas, NV
21 November 2021